Everyone's favorite amateur sleuth, Philomela Nightingale, and her husband, Brent Lark, plan to move to the seaside town of Saltaire. Realtors show them many houses, trying to find one that suits their tastes, needs, and budget. Occasionally, Philomela works in her sister's ladies' wear shop, and Procne appreciates the help, especially after two of her acquaintances are found strangled. Brent does his utmost to keep Philomela from prying into the two murders, but when work requires him to go to Saskatchewan, she becomes entangled in saving the life of a potential third victim. Will she succeed or will she become a victim herself?

KUDOS for *Saltaire Strangler*

In *Saltaire Strangler* by Benni Chisholm, Philomela Nightingale and her husband have moved to the quaint Canadian seaside village of Saltaire. No sooner do they get there and find a house to buy when their realtor is murdered. Philomela's husband tries to keep her from getting involved in the investigation, but when work takes him out of town, Philomela plunges headfirst into trying to find the killer. But she may find more than she bargained for…Written in Chisholm's unique and re-freshing voice, the story is fast paced, suspenseful, and full of surprises. A great read. ~ *Taylor Jones, The Review Team of Taylor Jones & Regan Murphy*

Saltarie Strangler by Benni Chisholm is the third book in her Philomela Nightingale Mystery series. This time, Philomela has sold her magazine business and she and her husband have moved to the small town of Saltaire in Canada. The seaside community is close knit and fairly quiet—until someone starts strangling women. When the realtor who sold Philomela and her husband, Brent, their new house is murdered, Brent is adamant that Philomela not interfere in the investigation. And she agrees, until he is called out of town. Then all bets are off, and Philomela finds herself fearing for her own life, as well as that of her family and friends. *Saltaire Strangler*, like the two books before it, is a well-written, fast-paced mystery with a cast of delightful and interesting characters, a solid plot, and plenty of twists and turns. I couldn't put it down. ~ *Regan Murphy, The Review Team of Taylor Jones & Regan Murphy*

ACKNOWLEDGMENTS

Thanks to the capable people at Black Opal Books. Your dedication and skillful help is much appreciated.

Thanks also to Shellie Park for solving my mysterious computer problems.

SALTAIRE

STRANGLER

Benni Chisholm

A Black Opal Books Publication

Black Opal Books

BECAUSE SOME STORIES JUST HAVE TO BE TOLD

GENRE: MYSTERY-DETECTIVE/WOMEN SLEUTHS/SUSPENSE

This is a work of fiction. Names, places, characters and incidents are either the product of the author's imagination or are used fictitiously, and any resemblance to any actual persons, living or dead, businesses, organizations, events or locales is entirely coincidental. All trademarks, service marks, registered trademarks, and registered service marks are the property of their respective owners and are used herein for identification purposes only. The publisher does not have any control over or assume any responsibility for author or third-party websites or their contents.

DEDICATION

To FMC and our amazing 66 years together.

CHAPTER 1

Wednesday Morning

Philomela Nightingale was annoyed. Glancing at her husband's clenched jaw, she knew he was experiencing a stronger emotion—exasperation. For thirty minutes they had waited patiently. Then, not so patiently, they had waited for another fifteen minutes. After forty-five minutes their initial house-hunting enthusiasm dropped from ten to zero.

Philomela rapped her knuckles on the locked front door of the house—for the fourth time. For the fourth time no one answered. For the second time, she strode to the back of the house and banged her fist on the locked door. For the second time no one responded.

She returned to the front of the house, peered through a large window at two attractive sofas, one coffee table, and two end tables. On the floor of an archway she noted a woman's black shoe. It crossed her mind that the owner must be careless and untidy.

Her stomach grumbled and she glanced at her wristwatch—eleven-fifty-five. Their meeting had been scheduled to start fifty-five minutes ago.

Brent harrumphed and she watched him march down the curving front path, stride across the public sidewalk to the curb, and climb behind the steering wheel of his one-ton Chevrolet truck. Her low-heeled walking shoes slowly followed his footsteps then veered to the passenger side of the vehicle. She climbed inside and sat down beside him.

For five minutes they sat and said nothing.

Then, like champagne from a newly uncorked bottle, Brent's exasperation erupted into full anger. "If that bloody realtor doesn't want to show us this house, I'm outa here." He snapped the ignition key and the engine spurted to life.

Suppressing her own annoyance, Philomela tried to lighten the mood. "Kathy may have been caught in heavy traffic."

"Heavy traffic in Saltaire?" Brent snorted. "Her license should be rescinded."

Philomela inhaled deeply and wondered why Kathy Holmes was forfeiting a chance to show a nice house to serious buyers. Slowly exhaling, she recalled yesterday afternoon when Kathy had shown them pictures of several attractive houses, pleasantly served them tea, and efficiently made an appointment for this morning's showing.

So, why did she fail to appear? Worse, why didn't she phone with an excuse for her absence?

CHAPTER 2

Wednesday Afternoon.

Philomela wondered about her own motives for house hunting. Did she have a chaotic desire to go through the hassle of moving? No. Would leaving her Calgary home and magazine job be a reasonable change? Not necessarily. Did she want to own a house and live in the town of Saltaire? Yes, because its temperate climate would be pleasant for retirees and also because her kid sister lived here.

Brent's foot pressed the accelerator and the truck sped forward. As it moved toward the Seaside Motel, Philomela tightened her lips and watched for police. All they needed to complete their morning angst was to get a speeding ticket.

Fortunately, it didn't happen.

Inside the motel room, she plopped onto a straight back chair and watched her husband's fingers jab the phone number of Trust Realty.

"I'd like to speak with Kathy Holmes." Much to her surprise, he spoke politely. A moment later his brows furrowed, and his voice matched his expression. "Annette, Kathy was supposed to meet us at eleven this morning.

We waited over an hour." He listened briefly then, almost rudely, said, "If she's one of the best realtors in town, why didn't she phone to apologize for her no-show?" He again listened, his lips pursed, and he muttered, "Okay, if he insists, put him on."

Realizing Brent no longer spoke with the person named Annette, Philomela wondered if Tom Trust, owner of the real estate company, was on the other end. Whoever it was must have been diplomatic and soothing for her husband grew slightly mollified.

He finally pressed the off button and turned to Philomela. "That was Roger Arthur Thistle, another realtor. He promised to contact Kathy and phone back."

A few minutes later Roger fulfilled the last half of his promise—he phoned back. Listening to Brent's side of the conversation, Philomela suspected the first half of Roger's promise remained unfulfilled.

Brent turned to Philomela and confirmed her suspicion. "Roger was unable to contact Kathy. She failed to answer her cellphone or her landline. He offered to help us. Do you want to go back to that house?"

"Might as well." To her own ears her voice sounded tired and dejected. Trying to be more optimistic, she said, "The exterior was nice."

"Okay Roger. We'll meet you tomorrow morning at ten-thirty…sharp." Brent shut off his phone.

A light lunch increased their blood sugars and their spirits. An afternoon nap alleviated the exhaustion that had been created by their descent from Calgary's 3500 foot altitude to Saltaire's sea level. By six p.m. they cheerfully sipped Chardonnay and prepared to watch the local news.

The TV newscaster immediately caught their attention.

"The Saltaire police are contacting a female realtor's next of kin. Late yesterday afternoon the realtor went alone to an empty house to meet an unknown client. This afternoon another realtor found her body inside the house. Her death is considered a homicide."

"Good grief!" Philomela's fingers gripped the stem of her glass and her abdominal muscles tightened. "Could the victim be Kathy Holmes?"

"I hope not," Brent replied.

As the newscaster left the topic of murder and droned on about the weather, Philomela recalled yesterday afternoon.

After she and Brent had enjoyed tea and conversation with Kathy Holmes, they had enthusiastically made a date for this morning's viewing. Back at the motel, Philomela had read several chapters of her mystery novel while Brent drove his truck to a nearby service station. On his return he had complained that a long line-up at the gas pumps had delayed him.

Why did that unimportant incident fill her mind right now?

CHAPTER 3

Thursday Morning

Philomela gazed up at the blue dome and squinted at the eastern sun. The weather was perfect—not too hot, not too cold. She stretched her arms above her head and murmured, "Brent, this is what locals call 'a ho-hum day in Paradise.'"

"That depends."

Ignoring his reference to yesterday's unpleasantness, she breathed in the soft moist air. The fascinating aroma of salt and fish pleasantly assailed her nostrils. Turning onto Main Avenue she realized the gentle ocean smells were blending with appetizing ones from a nearby bakery. She sniffed appreciatively and felt a pang of hunger. Anticipation of breakfast combined with the exercise of walking and the inhalation of soft fresh air helped her forget yesterday's heated emotions. Inside the History Café, the owner's cheery voice lifted her spirits even higher.

"Philomela, how nice to see you again. And you must be Brent. I'm Jean Greenfield, owner of this classy joint. Procne says you are the best brother-in-law ever."

Though appearing embarrassed, Brent chuckled. "Pleased to meet you, Jean. I hear you make the best fish chowder in town."

"Whoever told you that is a purveyor of truth." She handed menus to them both.

Philomela nodded and glanced at several empty tables. She moved to the closest one and sat down. Brent sat down across from her.

"Would you like coffee?" Jean asked.

"Yes, please," they replied in unison then grinned at each other.

Sipping their caffeinated brews, Brent chose the traditional Eggs Benedict and Philomela decided on the west coast version—salmon instead of ham. They gave their orders, glanced around the almost empty café, and quietly discussed its friendly ambience. They avoided talking about four subjects—leaving their current home, dealing with local realtors, settling in the town of Saltaire, and homicide.

The lack of these particular subjects helped them enjoy breakfast.

Finally, Philomela brought up two of the avoided items—realtors and homicide. "Why do you think Kathy Holmes was killed?"

"We don't know if she was killed," Brent corrected.

Philomela nodded, acknowledging his correction, but her abdomen clenched in negation. Her female intuition told her that Kathy was the murder victim. Holding her warm coffee mug in both hands, she gazed up at the ceiling and wondered if the realtor's body had been inside the house while she and Brent had waited impatiently outside. Visualizing the one black shoe in the archway she concluded it had belonged to Kathy.

At ten-twenty-eight, the red Chevrolet truck stopped near the FOR SALE sign in front of the house. Philomela contrasted yesterday morning's long wait for the realtor with today's prompt presence of Roger Thistle. He greeted them as they climbed from Brent's truck and pointed to the yellow police tape. His facial expression lacked any obvious emotion.

"Kathy Holmes was choked by a garrote of some sort. No one knows why, or by whom, or at what time."

Philomela shuddered. "So, the victim really was Kathy." She promptly recalled the young woman's vibrant personality, cheery outlook, slim figure, and attractive features. Then she thought of the realtor's family who now must be in total shock. There seemed to have been no inkling that Kathy had been plagued with serious problems or real enemies.

"Do the police have any suspects?" Brent stared questioningly at Roger.

"Not that I know of," he replied. "Obviously I can't show this house now. It's a crime scene. Who knows when the yellow tapes will come down?"

"In two or three days." Philomela spoke with authority.

Roger's eyebrows shot up in surprise. "Are you familiar with crime scenes?"

"Yes. I've been involved with a few." She waved her right hand as if sloughing off an unimportant statement. In actual fact, within the last seven years she had helped solve five murders. Brent complained that she attracted murders like a magnet attracted nails. At the moment she was inclined to agree with him.

"Murder is not my specialty," Roger said. "I took education at university, but I prefer real estate to teaching a bunch of youngsters. Early this morning, Corporal Stinson and Constable James came to the Trust Realty office. They quizzed all of us and took fingerprints, even though they doubted the killer's prints will be on anything. Constable James suspects the perpetrator wore gloves."

Philomela recognized the names of the police. She had met them in January, a year and a half ago, while visiting her sister. Three days after her arrival, the owner of two ladies shops had been fatally stabbed inside the Historical museum. Because of the unfortunate incident, Procne ended up purchasing the funky shop and Sheila Trust, wife of the owner of Trust Realty, bought the upscale one.

Thinking of the affable Constable James, Philomela recollected how Procne had referred to her as Dickless Tracy. Procne had insisted that the cartoon-based moniker was not derisive, but Philomela had wondered and still wondered if Constable James would agree.

Roger interrupted her rumination by getting back to the business at hand. "A similar house is for sale only a block away. Follow me and I'll take you there."

Philomela sat beside Brent who drove his red truck behind Roger's gray car. After parking on the driveway of a two-story house, they followed him into the dining, living, and kitchen areas. Roger showed them a TV room adjacent to a full bathroom and explained that in case of illness the two rooms could be used as a main floor ensuite bedroom. Upstairs they saw a master bedroom with a spacious bathroom, a guest bedroom adjacent to a tiny bathroom, and a small room that could be used as an office. The ocean view from upstairs was more expansive than the view downstairs.

Philomela found the house appealing. The only unappealing feature was the cost. It was well beyond their budget.

"I like this place," Brent said to Roger. "But the price is too high for our limited savings account. We need to inspect a few less expensive houses."

Roger smiled politely. "Of course. I'll take you to another house right now. The owners are away for two weeks. It's near the marina."

Brent and Philomela climbed into Brent's half-ton truck and followed Roger to a lovely district with large, spectacular houses. Nearby, tall masts on sailboats bobbed in a secluded bay. The boats added interest to the water view, especially for two city folks who were used to wide plains and rolling foothills.

The house Roger showed them was well planned and attractive, but much larger than they needed or wanted. The cost also exceeded their budget.

Philomela studied Roger. Had he not heard Brent ask to see less expensive houses?

CHAPTER 4

Thursday Noon

Roger glanced at his watch. "Look at the time. I'll buy you lunch at the Yacht Club."

"Oh, that would be nice." Philomela tried to sound suave though she felt a twinge of unsophisticated excitement. Strolling near the lake behind Glenmore Dam in Calgary couldn't compare with dining in a restaurant next to the big Pacific Ocean. Besides, she had never been in a real Yacht Club before.

"Just follow me," Roger said.

The two house hunters again climbed into Brent's truck and again trailed behind Roger's gray car. After Brent eased the truck into a large parking lot, they climbed outside and followed the realtor into a big, white, two-story building. Roger signed a sheet of paper sitting on a small table then led them up a short stairway.

Philomela gazed out a window. Two huge trees bordered each side of a pretty water view. She thought the trees were Cedar, but she wasn't sure. Seeing sailboats glide on the water, she recalled Procne describing such boats as rag-flyers. A silly name for crafts with attractive sails puffed out in a gentle breeze.

"There are four marinas around Saltaire," Roger said. "All are kept busy. A lot of the boats never move, but during the summer lots do. In the nice weather boaters from away are a common sight—sailing out on the water and eating and shopping in the town." He gazed at his clients and hospitably said, "How about a libation? A beer, a glass of wine?"

Philomela chose a six-ounce Okanagan Chardonnay.

Brent voiced his concern about drinking and driving then added, "Oh well, maybe I can handle half a pint of Herman's."

They walked with Roger to a bar and glanced at the name tag of the lady who stood behind it. "Belle, I'd like a six-ounce glass of chardonnay and two half pints of Herman's."

They picked up the glasses from the counter and Roger suggested they go outside to a deck. At a table warmed by the sun and sheltered from the ocean breeze by a glass barrier, they sat down.

Philomela sipped her white wine, breathed in the soft air, and studied one of the big trees. Its trunk was so large she knew she couldn't circle her arms around it. She was aware of conversation floating from a white-haired couple sitting at the adjacent table. Their cheerful words and the deck's overall ambience made her feel all was right with the world.

"This is lovely," she said to Roger. "I'd love to live in this area." To Brent she asked, "Could we afford to buy a house here?"

"Not likely. I fear their prices will exceed our budget." Brent glanced to Roger for confirmation but Roger seemed not to hear him. Turning his gaze to Philomela,

Brent raised his eyebrows questioningly. "If we move to Saltaire, will you miss your magazine?"

"Probably. At first. But I could keep my fingers in the pot by writing a few articles for Janice."

Brent explained to Roger that Philomela was the editor and publisher of a small magazine called 'The Integrator.' He added, "She's in the process of selling it to her stalwart employee."

"There are a few local magazines in our area," Roger said, and his gaze shifted from Brent to Philomela. "You could write articles for one of them."

"Perhaps I could. Then again, I may want a complete change—like taking up gardening, pottery, or gourmet cooking."

"Gourmet cooking?" Brent guffawed. "That I would like to see."

Philomela, who occasionally enjoyed cooking, grinned and changed the subject. "Brent plans to continue working part time in Calgary. At least for a short while."

Roger looked a query at Brent. "What do you do for a living?"

"I'm an engineer. A partner and I own a small oil company. The industry is in the doldrums right now. Between low prices, government disinterest, and ecological concerns, the industry stumbles along. It always surprises me that politicians and ecologists fly so often to interesting places around the world and simply forget that jet fuel comes from oil."

"Maybe they think the airplanes have Angelic wings."

Philomela giggled, surprised to find that Roger actually had a sense of humor.

"It could happen that a larger company will try to buy us out," Brent said.

Roger nodded. "That happens to a lot of small, successful businesses."

"Have you worked for Tom Trust very long?" Philomela asked.

"I've been with Trust Realty for seven months."

"Tom and his wife Sheila live in the same townhouse complex as my sister. Tom's president of their strata council."

"Really? I didn't know that." Roger brought out his cellphone, punched in some numbers and held it to his ear. "This is Roger Thistle with Trust Realty. I have clients who would like to see your house. Would it be possible to see it today between one and one-thirty?" He listened for a few seconds then said, "That's perfect." He shut off his cellphone and glanced at his wristwatch. "I just made arrangements to see another house. The owners will be gone for a couple of hours."

A waitress appeared and took their orders. Several minutes later she set their food on the table.

Philomela nibbled on Halibut and French fries. "It's true," she said. "Freshly-caught fish tastes better than freshly-frozen fish. This halibut doesn't smell even faintly fishy."

Expecting her husband to pick up on her excessive alliteration, she looked sideways at him. Instead of mentioning her many words starting with F, he quietly munched on a large hamburger.

She swallowed a few more bites then said, "This particular prairie person could easily become a true seafood lover." Suddenly her interest in fish was distracted by the words of the white-haired woman at the next table.

"I understand Kathy Holmes was dating Melvin Springer."

Philomela's ears perked up and she surreptitiously leaned toward the speaker.

"Really?" The man sounded surprised. "You mean Melvin's involved with another murder?"

"Involved, yes. But don't forget, Melvin was cleared of killing his wife."

"Well, he was a suspect for a while. You know the old chestnut—where there's smoke, there's fire."

CHAPTER 5

Thursday Afternoon

Roger led Philomela and Brent along a twisty road up to a house on top of a hill. The house was located on half an acre on the outskirts of town. It had a more expansive ocean view than the other houses they had seen and also had the bonus of being on one level. Stairs were no trouble now, but Philomela knew that arthritis or some other autoimmune disease might make stairs a problem in the distant future. Brent was unconcerned with the house—he was too enamored with the spacious two car garage.

"Would three vehicles fit in here?" Brent asked Roger.

Philomela knew what he was thinking. His 1965 Jaguar S-type would take priority over her Chevrolet Spark and his half-ton Chevrolet truck.

"Rather snug," Roger replied, "unless the vehicles are small."

"This is the best house yet," Brent said.

Philomela asked Roger the price and when he replied she groaned. "Pretty high. But I guess we have to pay extra for the ocean view and the double garage."

"Do you want to come back to the office and look through the multiple listings?" Roger asked. "You might find something else that suits you."

Philomela recollected looking at the multiple listings with Kathy Holmes. "I suppose the lists change every day."

"New listings and sold houses are marks of the trade. If you see something pleasing, I could arrange viewings for tomorrow."

"I'll not be able to house-hunt tomorrow morning," Philomela said. "I promised to look after my sister's shop while she visits her dentist. She owns Whimsical Woman."

"Procne? Procne Ellis?" Roger's eyebrows arched in surprise. He stared at Philomela. "You and Procne are sisters?"

"Amazing, isn't it."

"You don't look a bit alike."

Philomela nodded her head. "My red hair and short stature contrast sharply with her dark hair and gorgeously tall, slim figure."

"They do indeed." Then Roger diplomatically conceded, "But both are attractive."

"Thank you. You're very kind."

With little ado, Philomela and Brent followed Roger back to the real estate office. As they entered the reception area a young lady looked up from her computer and smiled.

"Hello. I'm Annette Murphy. I talked with you on the phone yesterday."

Looking contrite, Brent slowly moved his head from side to side. "Annette, I apologize for my abruptness. I was upset…not knowing what had happened to Kathy Holmes."

"Understandable." Annette gave him a wan smile. "Under any conditions, waiting for over an hour would be too frustrating for words."

"Have they found anything more about her death?" Philomela asked.

"Not that I've heard." Annette turned to the ringing phone, picked it up, and said, "Trust Realty."

"Please follow me." Roger's voice rang with impatience.

At his desk, Philomela and Brent sat down and faced their realtor. Under his tutelage they studied pictures and blurbs about houses costing well above their price range.

"I wonder if we'll ever find a house in Saltaire we can afford," Philomela murmured.

"You can always make an offer lower than the asking price," Roger said.

They chose a few houses of minor interest then made a date to meet Roger tomorrow afternoon.

CHAPTER 6

Shortly before six p.m. Brent and Philomela left the Seaside Motel. Philomela admired several flower gardens as they leisurely walked to her sister's townhouse. Philomela pressed the doorbell and Procne buzzed them into the open-air vestibule. Several seconds later she opened the door of her home.

"Welcome to my abode. You're just in time to help make dinner."

"I thought it was my night not to cook." Philomela gave her sister a mock frown. "Did you have to work late?"

"Yes, a few minutes. I always have chores to do after closing the store."

Brent greeted his sister-in-law with a quick hug then strolled to the living area.

Philomela saw him settle comfortably on a sofa and pick up a fashion magazine. Wondering if the pictures and articles would interest him for long, she entered the kitchen with her sister. In no time she started peeling carrots. Gazing at three white filets that Procne was preparing, she chuckled.

"Now I know I'm at the west coast—fish once yesterday and twice today." She proceeded to tell Procne about her fresh fish and chips at lunch and about her fish chowder yesterday. She then described the houses she and Brent had toured with Roger. Their conversation soon veered from the housing market to the recent murder.

"Kathy found this townhouse for me," Procne said. "She often came into the shop and I loved her taste in clothes. She always looked smashing. She told me she tried to portray an image of being both knowledgeable and successful. To her, knowledgeable meant looking intellectual and successful meant appearing well groomed. To enhance her wise appearance, she sometimes wore horn-rimmed glasses, though I don't think her eyes needed help. A couple of times we sat together at business women's lunches. She was lots of fun and interesting to talk with."

"Do you have any idea who might have strangled her?"

Procne shook her head. "I knew very little of her personal life. She wasn't married—divorced, I think. No children. I don't think she had a live-in partner, but I don't know for sure."

"Was she heterosexual?"

"Does that matter?" Procne dipped the fish in egg and flour.

"Not really. Today I overheard two ladies at lunch imply she and Melvin Springer were dating. I wondered if they had a serious relationship."

"I saw them together a couple of time, too. But I don't think they were seriously committed."

"I wonder if the murderer was angry with Kathy because of something she had said or done." Philomela frowned. "Perhaps the perpetrator's brain was full of imagined slights."

"Will we ever know?" Procne asked.

"I hope so, eventually." Philomela closed her eyes, visualized the young realtor, and said, "When we dealt with Kathy, she was attractive in appearance and pleasant in personality. She maintained a mild manner and she spoke softly."

Procne studied her sister and grinned.

"What's so funny?"

"Philomela, your addiction for alliteration is still intact."

Thinking of her recent words, Philomela chuckled. "I guess you're right. Attractive in appearance, pleasant in personality, maintained a mild manner, spoke softly—all in two short sentences. Oops there goes another one. Oh well. Right now, I only hope the person who attacked Kathy is brought to justice."

"Me too. Knowing a murderer is on the loose makes me nervous. And I'm not the only one who feels that way. Every woman in town feels the same, especially those who live alone."

When dinner was ready, Brent walked from the living room and joined the two women. Sitting at the dining table, all three ate and chatted amicably about Procne's dress shop, expensive housing in Saltaire, and Brent's 1965 Jaguar.

"I'd liked to find a house with a garage big enough to keep the Jag and Philomela's car under cover. I don't care so much about my truck. It's a work vehicle and has been used extensively in the field. It's already withstood all kinds of weather."

Procne glanced from her brother-in-law to her sister and her lips broke into a wide smile. "I'm so glad you two are going to retire here. I know you'll like it. And I'll certainly like having you nearby."

"Maybe we're making a mistake," Brent said. "Do people get killed in Saltaire on a regular basis?"

"Of course not." Two lines between Procne's eyebrows registered indignation. "The last person murdered here was Maxine Springer. A year and a half ago." She shivered and took a deep breath. "Her husband, Melvin, was so distraught he went to Arizona for three months. He rented his Saltaire house to a couple from the prairies. The murder didn't faze them, probably because they were happy to get away from temperatures of thirty degrees below freezing."

"I wouldn't want to live in a house recently vacated by a murdered victim," Philomela mused. "I'm sure I'd feel bad vibrations hanging in the air and clinging to the walls."

"This morning Selene said the same thing." Procne gazed benignly at her sister. "You may not be as psychic as my neighbor, but you both are sensitive to a lot of weird things. Melvin isn't sensitive like that. He's quite earthy and probably likes living with Maxine's things. He had trouble at first, but he's doing well now. He admitted to being relieved when Sheila and I bought Maxine's shops."

"I wonder if he'll ever truly get over the horror of his wife's death." Philomela glanced at Brent.

He raised his eyebrows and turned to his sister-in-law. "Procne, don't you think it strange that Philomela was in town for Maxine's murder? And now she's here in town for Kathy's?" Moving his head from side to side he pensively added, "I don't like it."

"I know you worry about her associating with dangerous killers," Procne said.

"And you're right, she could get hurt. Or worse…get killed."

"Good grief! You two are a couple of fusspots. Why would I become involved with Kathy's murderer? I know nothing about Kathy except what Roger Thistle, Annette, and you, Procne, have told us. I have no reason to become involved with her dreadful demise or with her killer."

"I'll remember those words." Brent's brown eyes focused on Philomela's green ones.

CHAPTER 7

Thursday Evening, Later

After Philomela and Brent left the townhouse to walk back to the Seaside Motel, Procne tidied up her kitchen. Plopping on one of the high stools, she leaned her elbows on the eating counter and thought about the deceased realtor. Kathy's murder had shocked everyone, especially those who knew her. There seemed no rhyme or reason for her untimely death. She did her job well and was considerate of everyone in the process.

Why, Procne wondered, would anyone in his or her right mind want Kathy dead? Procne sat up straight and asked herself, "Is that a pertinent clue? Was the murder committed by someone not in his or her right mind?" Oh dear, she was getting as bad as Philomela.

She knew Brent worried about Philomela being in town when this murder was committed. And Procne agreed with Brent.

Her sister had been on hand when murders were committed in Maui, Calgary, and twice in Saltaire. It was very strange. Was it a coincidence that Philomela and Brent had arrived in town the day before Kathy was murdered? Had fate played a part in their choice of realtor?

Could Philomela be destined to help the police solve another murder? Procne shook her head. She couldn't analyze it. The entire situation was too weird to think about.

But she continued to think about it. She knew her sister well—Philomela was even tempered, steady, thoughtful, and usually behaved in a logical manner even when others didn't. She saw a glass half full when others saw it half empty. And she had an amazing knack to help fix things. The knack extended beyond fixing minor problems. It extended to major problems such as solving murders.

In a manner of speaking, Philomela and Selene Hamilton were similar yet complete opposites. Both were sensitive to other people's feelings. Procne's psychic neighbor, however, foretold happenings, both good and bad, whereas Philomela helped repair bad happenings after they had surfaced. Selene had explained that her empathy and prophetic ability were gifts from God that helped her solve distraught people's problems before they got worse. Procne wasn't sure if Philomela treated her intuition and gut feelings as a gift from God or as a gift from the subconscious, but she did know that Philomela had helped justice to be served after serious actions had occurred.

Procne jumped down from the stool and in a spur of the moment decision picked up the phone. When Selene's soft, gentle voice answered, Procne asked if she could pop next door for a quick chat.

"Certainly, Procne. I'm alone and I have no commitments."

"I'll come right over."

Inside Selene's townhouse, the two of them sat on one of Selene's blue and white loveseats and sipped herb tea.

"Selene," Procne said, twisting her head toward her neighbor. "Did you know Kathy Holmes very well?"

"She came to me a couple of times for tarot card readings. I believe you recommended me to her."

"Yeah, I did. She wanted advice about her personal life. There was a man…"

"A couple of men," Selene said.

Procne's ears twitched. "She only mentioned one man to me and I gathered he was more of a nuisance than a lover or a friend. That's when I suggested she contact you."

Selene gazed up at the ceiling. When she finally spoke, her words came slowly. "I can tell you the gist of her search for answers. After she visited me, she sent a particular man to see me. I pointed out that he was infatuated with her success as a realtor, not with her as a person. Once that was brought to his attention, he admitted it was probably true. He was a car salesman and ended up moving to Vancouver. I understand he is very successful. I don't think he's the murderer."

"Too bad. I was hoping we might solve the case. I think I met him last year at the Summer Solstice party at the Community Centre, but I'm not sure. That particular evening Basil Devonshire latched onto Cathy and they did a few credible Tangos together. I thought maybe the salesman might be jealous enough to kill one or both of them."

"My goodness, no." Selene shook her head emphatically.

"A couple of other fellows hung around her…one was tall and the other was her height…I didn't pay enough attention." Procne sighed.

Selene took a sip of tea, again glanced up at the ceiling then looked directly at Procne. "As far as Kathy's death is concerned, I'm in the dark. The murderer could be anyone."

"Anyone except you or me." Procne exposed her teeth in a brief grin. "I might talk with Tom Trust. He was the one who directed Philomela and Brent to Kathy. He said she was the best residential realtor in town. Tom, of course, deals more with the business side of his real estate firm."

"Who will your sister and brother-in-law deal with now?"

"A realtor by the name of Roger Thistle offered to help them. He works in Tom's office. I met him briefly at a business lunch, at a cocktail party, and once at the Town Cinema, but I don't really know him. Philomela and Brent seem impressed with him. He took them to the Yacht Club for lunch."

"Nice. Will Kathy's murder affect your sister and brother-in-law's decision to retire here?"

"I hope not. They saw three houses today. All were beyond their financial means. Roger is going to search out others for them."

A black cat jumped on Selene's lap. Her fingers gently stroked the hair on his back and she asked, "Well, Hecate, what do you think? Will Kathy's murder affect Philomela's and Brent's decision to buy here? And will the murderer be found quickly?"

Procne heard the cat start to purr. She wondered if somehow he was answering Selene's two questions.

CHAPTER 8

Friday Morning

The bell tingled as Philomela walked into the ladies' shop. She closed the door and looked at her sister who was busy behind the cash counter.

"What kept you?" Procne asked.

"Nothing much. Have you been here long?"

"I've been here for hours...well...half an hour. I've already vacuumed and put the float in the cash desk."

"Such efficiency. Do you always come to work early?"

"I clean and get a lot of paperwork done before customers arrive. Yesterday I managed to put some new winter stock on display. Do you want to examine it? The dresses, tops, and pants are very nice. They're hanging on that new arrival rack." She pointed to the rack nearest the door. "A few new sweaters are on the shelves. As you know, jewelry is displayed on the counter and scarves hang beside it."

"You haven't changed the layout since I was last here."

"There's no point in fixing something that doesn't need fixing. Maxine really had everything well organized."

"Yes, she did." Philomela stepped up to the new arrival rack and flicked through the merchandise. Hearing the door tingle, she looked over at it.

Two women entered the shop. One, a lady of indeterminate age, immediately walked to the back of the shop and studied garments on the sale rack. The other lady, obviously younger, walked toward the cash counter where Procne was putting away papers. Philomela recognized her as the pianist and master of ceremonies at Maxine's memorial fashion show a year and a half ago.

"Hi, Rebecca," Procne said. "How are you?"

"Very well, thanks. But unfortunately, I'm here to buy a funeral outfit."

"For Kathy Holmes?"

Rebecca nodded.

"Maybe you should talk to Sheila at Upscale Garments. As you know, she specializes in black and white."

"I don't want to be a traditional mourner. I want to remember Kathy as the high-spirited, cheerful person she was."

"Well then, you've come to the right shop."

Rebecca leaned toward Procne and said in sotto voice, "Besides, Whimsical Woman's clothes are cheaper than Upscale Garments'."

Procne chuckled. "True."

"Kathy lived next door to me. I can't believe she's dead, let alone murdered." Rebecca shuddered. "And in such a horrid way. Probably by a nut case."

Procne nodded.

"She was a wonderful neighbor. Lots of fun. Outgoing and hard working. She was dedicated to her realtor job."

Procne nodded again.

Listening to Rebecca's words and noting her dark hair and tanned skin, Philomela plucked a navy dress with matching navy and pink jacket from the rack. She held them up. "Rebecca, would this dress suit you? It's a size medium."

"You remember my sister," Procne said. "Philomela."

"Of course. We ate lunch together at the memorial fashion-show."

"You did a fantastic job both as master of ceremonies and as pianist."

"Thank you. I admired Maxine so I was glad to participate in her final show."

Philomela handed the pink and navy outfit to her. "This is classy yet cheery."

Rebecca took hold of the outfit, held it up and studied it. She looked over at the shop owner. "What do you think, Procne?"

"The pink is cheery but not too flamboyant. Why don't you try it on?"

Rebecca chose two other dresses and went into one of the small dressing rooms.

Procne gave her sister a two-thumbs-up sign. "I'd better hire you as a saleslady."

Philomela grinned and felt a flush of success touch her cheeks. The flush increased when Rebecca actually purchased the pink and navy outfit. Philomela admitted to herself that working part time for her kid sister might be fun.

At ten-fifty a.m., Procne dashed out the door for her eleven o'clock appointment with the dental hygienist. Left in charge of the shop, Philomela chatted pleasantly with customers and sold two tops, one skirt, and a necklace.

Precisely at twelve noon, the bell on the door tingled and she watched a tall man stride inside. He looked vaguely familiar. She knew she should know him, but she couldn't come up with a name.

"Hello, Philomela. Are you enjoying your stay in our charming town?"

"Yes, I am." She studied him and wracked her brain. Who was he?

"Procne said you and your husband were coming to house hunt. Have you found a place yet?"

"No, we haven't." Then she blurted out the ugly truth: "Our first realtor was murdered."

"Oh my god, Kathy Holmes." His nose scrunched, his jaw tightened, and his head moved from side to side. "Dreadful. She was a nice young woman, one of the best realtors in town. You'll need a replacement. Or have you already found one?"

"Roger Thistle. He also works at Trust Realty. He's pleasant enough and seems eager to help us."

"I'm sure he is. After all, a house sale means realtor fees for him." He grinned then glanced around. "Is Procne here?"

"No, she's at the dentist's office. She should be back soon."

"I promised to give her news about Angelina. Perhaps you recall my wife. She's in long term care at the hospital."

Now Philomela recognized him—Simon Fraser, curator of the Historical Museum. No wonder she didn't recognize him. He had aged since she saw him a year and a half ago. Doubtless he suffered considerable stress—his wife suffered from early onset Alzheimer's and the prognosis was grim. "How is Angelina doing?"

"Not too bad, all things considered. As expected, her illness is progressing."

"I'm sorry to hear that. I gather no real treatment is available, let alone a cure.

"Not yet."

Philomela dropped the depressing topic and asked, "Do you want me to have Procne phone you?"

"No, I'll be in and out of the museum all afternoon. I'll pop in again sometime after lunch. Basil Devonshire and I are going to grab a bite at the History Café."

Philomela recalled how Procne had given moral support to Simon after his wife was first admitted to hospital. She also knew her sister was fond of him. Watching him go out the door, she suspected the feeling was mutual. But as far as romance was concerned the situation seemed hopeless. Angelina and her illness stood firmly between them.

When Procne arrived back at the shop she held up a brown paper bag. "I bought lunch." She waved the bag high in the air. "Comfort food. It's probably unhealthy and full of unneeded calories and all sorts of other bad stuff."

"Oh well, I'm sure we'll survive." Philomela smiled. "Do you need any fillings or crowns?"

"None. My teeth are perfect, though still a bit crooked."

"That trait isn't noticeable." Philomela followed her sister to the office at the back of the shop and watched her set a plastic container of cherry tomatoes, a jar of green olives, and four sausage-rolls on the desk. "The pastry will have lots of gluten," Philomela said.

Procne looked at her sharply and asked, "You haven't developed gluten intolerance, have you?"

"No, thank goodness. By the way, you had a visitor today."

"Who?"

"Simon Fraser."

"Oh." Procne picked up a sausage-roll and with obviously feigned nonchalance asked, "What did he want?"

"He wanted to update you about his wife. He plans to pop back after lunch. He's eating lunch with Basil Devonshire at the History Cafe."

"That's nice."

"Speaking of Basil, how's his wife doing with her shopaholic symptoms?"

"Better. A couple of weeks ago Grace started to buy a sweater and I asked if she really needed it. She studied the sweater a minute and then shook her head and put it neatly back on the shelf."

"Good for her. And good for you, Procne. I'm sure you wanted to make the sale, but you gave her problem first priority."

"Yeah. Your kid sister isn't all bad." Procne grinned.

Philomela couldn't help but chuckle. She didn't consider Procne bad at all, perhaps a bit scatterbrained on occasion, but never bad.

True to his word, Simon returned to the shop about one-thirty. Philomela didn't purposely listen to their conversation but it was hard not to overhear it. Simon asked Procne if she would be free about six-thirty to help take his wife back to the hospital. "I'm bringing Angelina home for an early dinner," he explained, "but an unexpected emergency meeting came up with the Board of Directors at the museum. Seven p.m. was the only time slot available for everyone, so I have to adjust my plans to fit it. I plan to take her back to the hospital around six-thirty, but sometimes it takes a while to get her moving. Once she's settled, she doesn't want to go anyplace. If that happens and I have to rush off, I'd appreciate your help."

Procne didn't even glance at Philomela. "Of course, I'll help."

"Could you come to our house around six-fifteen?"

Procne nodded. "I'll eat an early dinner." She glanced at her sister who nonchalantly stood at a clothing rack adjusting items in the order of ascending sizes.

Simon strode to the door, paused and glanced back at Philomela, "Good luck to you and your husband in finding the perfect house."

CHAPTER 9

Friday Afternoon

Roger Thistle was ever the gentleman. After parking in front of a Trust Realty 'For Sale' sign, he opened the car door for Philomela. Inside the house, he pointed out a large en-suite master bedroom, a guest bedroom with adjoining bathroom, and a kitchen with new appliances including a wine fridge.

Philomela gazed out the kitchen window at a large ship docked at the ferry terminal. "I wouldn't get any work done. I'd even be more interested in the car ferries than in the wine fridge. And that's saying something."

Roger ignored her wine quip. "You'd get used to the view. And you'd be close to ferries in case you wanted to go shopping in Vancouver or go visiting on the mainland."

Brent nodded. "Yes, ferry terminal and airport have to be considered. Living on an island will be different from what we're used to. We won't be able to hop in the car on the spur of the moment and go for a road trip."

"Yes, you can," Roger said. "There are lots of interesting places to visit without leaving the island."

The next house he showed them was near the center of Saltaire, only four blocks away from Main Avenue. The house was two years old, had modern new appliances, and a trendy open plan.

Philomela liked it.

Brent had reservations. "A single garage. A small lot. No yard to speak of."

"Do you want a large yard?" Philomela studied his face. "I didn't know you were fond of gardening or cutting grass."

"That's because I'm too busy drilling and attending meetings to spend time gardening. Semi-retirement will be a new ballgame. I may like growing our own vegetables. I'll certainly like tinkering on my new old Jaguar."

Philomela snickered.

"You'll both enjoy retirement," Roger assured them, walking to his car. "All retirees out here are busy. They wonder how they ever had time to work."

"Now there's a worry," Brent said. "When I retire, I don't want to be busy." He climbed into Roger's car to go to a third house and asked if the police had come up with anything new about Kathy's murder.

"Not that I've heard," Roger replied.

"The longer it takes to find suspects," Philomela said, "the harder it will be to locate the killer."

Roger nodded. "I'm sure that's true."

By the end of the morning they had examined four houses. All four sat in nice locations, had practical attractive floor plans and contained big price tags. One jumped out at Philomela and seemed to holler, *I'm the one*. Unfortunately, Brent vetoed the house when he saw it had a one car garage and cost more than they could afford. Before Roger dropped them off at the Seaside Motel, they agreed to go out with him again on Sunday afternoon.

Inside their motel room, Philomela kicked off her shoes and flopped on the bed. House hunting certainly wasn't a ten, but it had eased up from zero to five. At least Roger hadn't kept them waiting. Besides being prompt, he was amicable and seemed to have no enemies. But Kathy Holmes also had been amicable and seemed to have no enemies.

"I'm hungry," Brent said.

She sat up and dropped her legs over the side of the bed. "Let's go to the History Café and have a snack. The food is good and Jean Greenfield is a fountain of information. She may have news about Kathy."

At the café, before Philomela brought up the important topic of murder, Jean said, "I recollect that you were a big help in finding Maxine Springer's killer. Maybe you'll be able to help the police solve Kathy's murder."

"I wouldn't count on it." Philomela modestly shook her head.

"How's the house hunting?" Jean asked, changing the subject.

"News spreads quickly." Philomela smiled, acknowledging that Saltaire was a small town rather than a big one. "Did you know our first realtor quite well?"

"I did." Jean shook her head. "A tragedy. A terrible tragedy. She was too young to die, especially in such horrid circumstances."

"Have you heard how the case is progressing?"

"Sergeant Stinson and Constable James were here this morning for coffee. If they knew anything, they weren't telling. Personally, I don't think they have a clue as to why she was killed or who did it."

"So, the murderer is still on the loose."

"Yes." Jean briefly pressed her lips together. "Everyone is edgy. We all wonder if there will be a next victim."

"Let's hope there isn't one."

"If there is one, who will it be?"

Philomela shook her head and peripherally saw Brent move away and stroll past tables, all of which were occupied. "Jean, you seem very busy."

"I hate to admit it, but everyone comes in here to learn about, and to discuss, the sad news. In the process, of course, they buy food and drinks."

"You're experiencing the silver lining of a cloudy happening."

"That's a nice way to describe it."

Philomela paid for two fish chowders and carried the bowls to a newly freed table for two that Brent had claimed. Setting the bowls on the table, she peripherally saw Sheila Trust enter the cafe. She turned and waved to the newcomer who promptly walked over to her. Philomela introduced her to Brent.

"How's the house hunting going?" Sheila asked him.

"It's going quite well. But Philomela is too fussy."

"Me? Fussy?" Philomela laughed. "It's the opposite, Sheila. Brent can't find a nice house with a huge garage."

"Be patient. I'm sure one will turn up."

"We were sorry to learn about Kathy Holmes," Philomela said.

Sheila's shoulders sagged. "Tom and I are dismayed by her death, as is everyone in town. She's a real loss for Tom. She was his best realtor and a nice person besides. He's also worried about the town's future, especially its real estate. He's afraid the murder will scare off prospective buyers. I hope you two don't feel that way. I understand you were waiting to meet with Kathy at the actual crime scene."

Philomela nodded. "Apparently her body was discovered shortly after we left. It's sad. I bet Kathy wasn't even thirty-five years old."

"Actually, she was forty."

"That's still too young to die—at any time or in any way." Noting Sheila's black pants and crisp white blouse, Philomela turned to a cheerier topic. "How's Upscale Garments? Is business booming?"

"It is. Summer was great, thanks to the tourists. And it's still booming. Procne's finding the same thing at Whimsical Woman. Neither of us regrets having accepted Maxine's posthumous offer to buy the shops. As business deals go, she was extremely generous."

Philomela nodded. "Maxine's was another sad death. But as the old cliché says, it's *an ill wind that bears no good.* You and Procne benefited. And now look at this busy café—for Jean the cliché is dead on." Philomela put her hand over her mouth. "Oops, that was a bad choice of words. I seem to have developed foot in mouth disease. I'll try again—Jean is benefiting from the onslaught of curiosity seekers."

Sheila glanced around at the tables full of customers. "True. Do you think the police will find Kathy's killer as fast as they found Maxine's?"

"I don't know. Jean Greenfield saw the police this morning and she said they didn't impart any information."

"Too bad." Sheila shrugged. "Well, I'd better eat and get back to the shop. I have a young woman attending it for a couple of hours. Nice to meet you, Brent." With a wave of her right hand, she strode to the counter, spoke briefly to the owner of the café, then sat down on the last empty stool at the counter overlooking Main Avenue.

Recalling Maxine Springer's body on the sofa in the Historical Museum, Philomela shuddered. Volunteer

Basil Devonshire had found Maxine's body and had been distraught. The victim's husband, Melvin Springer, had expressed anger at the world and had blamed everyone for her death before succumbing to sorrow. His life, of course, had been drastically changed. To date, he had never remarried, and as far as she knew, he was not cohabiting with another partner.

"So," Brent said, disturbing her rumination, "That was Tom Trust's wife. A classy looking lady."

"She should be. She has first dibs on hundreds of upscale garments."

"Do I detect a twinge of envy?"

"Perhaps. I'm only human. And I am female. Of course, I can always go to Whimsical Woman and Procne will give me thirty percent off."

"Is that all?"

"She has to pay rent, town and provincial taxes, water, electricity, gas, and hired help. She can't afford to give me free clothing."

"You seem to know more about the retail business than I ever suspected."

"I know as much as most, and more than many." She saw his eyes roll and his expression indicate "not again." Before he could mention her addiction, she said, "Okay, so I just abused alliteration."

He chuckled. "Maybe not abused, but certainly overused."

She couldn't help but smile. She wondered if her overuse of words starting with the same letter rose from a birthright, possibly in her genes, or from her tendency to write poetry. Then again, it could simply be a careless weakness in speech. Poets, of course, considered it a talent. Glancing at two ladies taking over the newly emptied adjacent table, she said, "How do you think our house hunting went today?"

"Interesting. The houses were nice but too expensive. Roger can't seem to show us anything we can afford."

"He suggested we could always make a lowball offer."

"Why bother. So far, we haven't even found anything we agree on. You're too fussy."

"Your expectations are too high. A three-car garage?" Seeing the twinkle in his eyes, she felt laughter roll from her throat to her mouth. It burst forth and felt good. She hadn't laughed like that since learning about Kathy Holmes's murder. When her laughter subsided, she scooped chowder onto a soup spoon and raised it to her mouth. She almost missed putting it between her lips because of being startled by the words of a lady at an adjacent table.

"I wondered about their relationship. He may have been her boss, but that didn't bother her. She was sexy and available, and seduction would be easy for her. Besides, his wife was busy, completely obsessed with her dress shop. He was an easy target for someone like—oh dear, I don't want to speak badly about the dead."

Philomela leaned sideways toward the speaker and pretended to concentrate on her food. She scooped up more chowder, swallowed, and listened intently.

"Speak softer," the second lady said. "His wife is sitting at the counter overlooking Main Avenue."

"I doubt that she can hear us." But the speaker took her friend's advice and started to whisper.

Leaning further sideways, Philomela tried to understand their quiet words. Then, with a yelp, she leaned too far and almost toppled off her chair. "Good grief!" she exclaimed, righting herself in awkward embarrassment. It took a few seconds to regain a semblance of composure and then she murmured to no one in particular, "I must be getting old. I seem to have a balance problem." Of course she didn't mention that her real problem was her failed effort to eavesdrop.

Seeing the two ladies stare at her, Philomela smiled innocently at them and turned to Brent who also stared at her. Though he didn't roll his eyes, he might as well have done so. She knew he realized she had behaved like a snoop, listening to a nearby conversation. She also knew her near fall would garner no sympathy from him. Nonchalantly as possible she resumed eating her chowder. But with every spoonful she still tried to hear more about Tom Trust and the deceased Kathy Holmes.

Unfortunately, the two ladies whispered below Philomela's hearing level.

CHAPTER 10

Friday Evening

S hortly after six-thirty p.m. Philomela's cellphone rang. It was Procne and she sounded flustered.

"Angelina insisted on staying in her comfortable chair and Simon didn't want to force her into his vehicle. Because he felt obligated to go to the museum's emergency meeting, I promised him I'd try and persuade her to go for a lovely car ride. So far, I haven't succeeded. Not being a knowledgeable caregiver, I wonder if you could come over and help me."

"Good grief, Procne, I know less than you do about caring for people with dementia. But I'll come. Perhaps Brent will come with me." She glanced at her husband who was watching the news on TV. "If we're lucky, Angelina may respond better to a man than to a female."

"Thanks. You're a lifesaver. Here's Simon's address."

Philomela wrote the address on a slip of paper then hung up the phone.

"Brent," she said, "Could you tear yourself away from the boob-tube to give Procne some moral support?" She explained the situation.

"Does she want us right now?"

"Yes. Extended care facilities ready their patients for bed quite early."

"Okay." He flicked off the TV.

Several minutes later, Philomela spotted Procne's white Mazda parked at the curb in front of a sand colored two-story house. Its roof tiles matched both Brent's red, half-ton Chevrolet truck and her vibrant red hair. As her husband parked behind the Mazda, Philomela studied the house. She liked its Mexican appearance and considered it appropriate—though the winter climate of northern Mexico was at least ten degrees warmer than Saltaire's.

As they walked up the front steps, Procne eagerly opened the door.

"Come on in." She led them into the living room and pointed to a device parked near a wingback chair. "Angelina has balance problems, so to prevent falls, she uses this walker. She also has a wheelchair, but it's at Sunset Wing."

Philomela stared at the woman sitting upright on the wingback chair. Her hair was held back at the nape by a fancy hairclip, her upper body was encased in a soft pink cardigan, and her eyes looked toward the picture window. She paid no attention to the newcomers, not until Philomela walked up to her.

"Hello, Angelina. I'm Philomela."

Angelina turned her head and stared blankly at Philomela. "I don't know you." Her abrupt words were softened by a sweet smile.

"I'm Procne Ellis's sister."

"Who's Procne Ellis?"

"She's right here." Philomela grabbed her sister's arm and pulled her forward.

"Hello," Procne said.

"Have we met?"

"Yes, we met at the museum."

"Museum? What museum?"

Philomela beckoned to Brent. He moved forward and as he stopped beside the woman's chair, Philomela said, "Angelina, this is Brent."

Angelina studied him a few seconds, cocked her head, and politely said, "I'm pleased to meet you."

"And I you. How are you feeling?"

"Fine, thank you. Are you fine, too?"

"Yes, I am."

Her eyes turned back to the picture window. "Look at the parade out there. I love parades."

Procne, Brent, and Philomela stared out the window at the two parked vehicles on the street.

"Where's the parade?" Procne whispered.

Angelina ignored Procne and looked directly at Philomela. "I once saw a man dig a hole and take someone out of it."

"Really?"

"Yes."

"Where is the hole?" Philomela asked.

"Near my new home. Oh...I do love parades."

"It's a nice day for a parade," Brent said. "Would you like to go outside for a better look? We could climb into that big red truck."

"Could we?" Angelina's eyes sparkled.

"Yes, we can go right now." Brent squatted in front of her "Would you like me to help you get up from the chair?"

Angelina nodded and Brent grasped both her hands. With his help, she put her feet flat on the floor, slid her buttocks out of the chair, and stood up. Like a gallant old-fashioned knight, he stood straight and tall and held out his curved arm. She automatically put her hand through the space between his body and his arm. Procne grabbed Angelina's leather purse from the wingback chair and took her other arm. The threesome walked to the front door and went outside.

Behind them, Philomela wheeled the walker down the front steps and watched Brent lift Angelina into the passenger seat. Angelina fussed a bit, apparently looking for something. Procne handed her the leather purse and, with nary a word, Angelina snatched it and placed it on her lap. Brent lifted the walker and put it in the back of the truck.

"Procne," he said, "you and Philomela lead the way in your Mazda, and I'll follow with Angelina. If I have any problems, I'll pull to the roadside and turn on my flashers."

Procne ran back to the Fraser house, locked the door, and returned to her car. She jumped inside and sat down behind the steering wheel. Glancing at her sister, she said, "Now I'll be able to go directly home from the hospital."

The drive to the hospital parking lot was short and uneventful. Brent eased into an empty spot beside the Mazda as Procne hurried to the ticket machine. Twice she inserted money and twice she snatched a ticket. She gave one to Brent who placed it on the truck's dashboard and she placed the other at the base of her car's front windshield.

Angelina rejected the walker and took Brent's right arm. Procne again helped by holding her left arm. They walked at each side of Angelina and sometimes almost carried her to the main entrance of the hospital. Philomela tagged behind, pushing the walker. The doors opened automatically and they went inside.

"Where to?" Brent asked Procne.

"Go straight then turn left."

After a few twists and turns they stopped in front of a closed door. Procne reached up, pressed a high green button, and the door opened. They walked half way down a long corridor. At a room containing two beds, Procne directed Brent to turn into it. The threesome passed a lady sitting in a chair beside the first bed and Procne guided Brent toward the second one.

"This is Angelina's area," she said.

Philomela gazed at the comfortable looking bed and noted a bedside table on which sat a bouquet of flowers and a stuffed dog. Several pictures were taped on a wall behind the bed. She glanced at Angelina who was looking around as if disoriented.

"Where are we?" she asked.

"In your room," Procne replied.

"Who are you?" Angelina glared at Procne and grasped Brent's arm.

"A friend," Procne replied.

"I don't know you."

"I'm Procne. I'm helping you."

"I don't need your help."

At that moment a nurse entered the room and smiled warmly. "Angelina, how nice to see you. Did you have a good time?"

Angelina clung to Brent's arm and stared at the nurse. "I don't know you."

"I'm Shannon," the nurse said. "I'm glad to see you looking so well."

With a puzzled expression, Angelina watched the nurse move a wheelchair close to her. Shannon adeptly guided Angelina into it and wheeled her over to the window.

"Here is your favorite place. You can look outside while I get your hot chocolate."

"Chocolate," Angelina said.

Shannon walked up to Brent. "I hope she was okay at home. "

"She was reluctant to leave, at first. Then she agreed."

The nurse nodded with obvious understanding. "After her hot chocolate I'll get her ready for bed. This is probably a good time for you to leave."

As Shannon disappeared out the door, Philomela and Procne moved toward it. Brent walked over to Angelina, kissed her cheek, and said, "Good night. Sweet dreams."

"I like chocolate." She smiled at him then looked out the window.

Going out the door, Philomela heard Angelina say to no one in particular, "That's where the hole is. The one that had a person in it."

The nurse returned with a mug of hot chocolate, smiled at them and said, "Goodnight."

When the threesome neared the main entrance, Philomela bent down and scooped up a piece of paper from the floor. "Litterbugs should be fined," she said. Glancing at the paper she stopped walking. "Good grief. This is interesting."

"What did you find?" Brent asked. "A hundred-dollar bill?"

"Something even better." She handed the paper to him.

He scanned it and his eyes widened. "Jaguar Club. They invite us to join. They have a phone number and an email address."

"How serendipitous that I have a fetish for tidiness."

"Fortunate indeed, Philomela." He folded the paper and tucked it into his breast pocket.

Outside the hospital, Procne thanked them. "Brent, you were amazing with Angelina. Way better than I was. I'd still be trying to get her to move from Simon's chair if you hadn't come over."

"It's my irresistible charm." Brent bowed in mock humility.

Philomela chuckled. "The female persuasion of all species are drawn to him like earthworms to soil."

Brent screwed up his nose at her. "I have to confess—the mother of a boyhood friend had early onset dementia. It was sad, but I learned from him to be kind and not be intimidated by the illness."

"Well, you obviously learned well," his sister-in-law said.

Philomela quizzically studied her sister then cleared her throat. "Procne, it's none of my business, but how long have you had a key to Simon's house?"

"Since six-fifteen this evening. I'll give it back to him tomorrow."

Though hoping to be subtle, Philomela's question indicated her interest in the attraction between Procne and Simon. Nothing more was said, but Philomela realized Angelina was still well ensconced between them.

Sitting beside Brent in his truck, Philomela thought about Simon's wife. "Early onset Alzheimer's is dreadful," she said. "Harder on the family than on the patient. Perhaps not at first, but certainly later. How awful it must be to watch a vibrant loved one disintegrate into a nonresponding vegetable."

Philomela knew Simon had coped with Angelina at home until her wanderings had brought things to a head. She had gotten lost more and more often and couldn't remember her home address or how to get there. Usually someone who knew her had brought her home. At first, she always wore shoes and a coat, but then one cold rainy day she went out without them. The police were called and the search was on. Hours later, two hardy hikers found her on top of a small hill in a nearby park. She was confused, cold, and hungry, so they took her to the local police station. Corporal Stinson recognized her and phoned Simon. Distraught, he arrived at the station and became even more distraught when she didn't know who he was. That incident forced him to seek the help of care-givers at home. Before long, it became obvious that a se-cure facility was the only solution. For the past year and a half, she deteriorated and he regularly visited her at the Sunset Wing.

Philomela's thoughts jumped from Angelina Fraser to Kathy Holmes. She tried to put the lives of the two wom-en in proper perspective.

Which was worse? Angelina's severe memory loss, resulting in a lengthy living death? Or Kathy Holmes's happy vibrant life shortened by a brutal death?

CHAPTER 11

Later Friday Evening

Philomela explained to Brent that the tourist town of Saltaire was widely known for its Friday evening summer street market. So, side by side they meandered from the motel to Main Ave and sauntered past the numerous tents. They tried to distinguish boaters wandering on shore from their boats, landlubbers strolling from their hotels and trailers, locals walking from their nearby homes, and other people who had driven from neighboring farms, acreages and towns.

Concluding it was a pointless pursuit, Philomela concentrated on fresh produce and crafty merchandise. In single file, they hurried past a thumping rock and roll group.

Brent spoke loudly over his shoulder. "They're a bit loud for me."

Philomela agreed. "We're members of the wrong generation."

A block later they stopped and listened to a quiet classical guitarist. They both considered him a talented musician. Further along, they enjoyed an excellent young pianist in a jazz quartet. Later they listened to and watched the nimble activity of a marimba group.

Philomela was amazed at a white plaster-man who in arabesque stood perfectly still. He didn't seem to breathe or blink his eyes. Philomela stared at him and began to suspect he was in fact a statue. Then someone dropped a coin in the bucket in front of him—and he winked, brought his back leg forward and did a brief dance. Then he resumed his motionless position. She wondered how anyone could stay so still for so long.

Holding her hand above her eyes to filter the setting sun, she cut through the crowd and caught up with Brent. They gazed at fresh farm vegetables and fruit, jewelry, soap, ceramics, fudge, cupcakes, gluten-free bread, earthquake information, and several outlets serving meals.

"The chowder at noon was good," she said, "but I'm hungry again. Let's grab a bite here at the market."

Brent studied the different vendors then stopped at a hotdog stand. "How about this one?"

"Very exotic." She giggled.

He quickly chose a Russian hotdog—a bun containing a wiener topped with relish and sauerkraut. With less speed she decided on a Canadian one. "Rather an odd mix," she said, picking up the serviette wrapped hotdog dripping with Maple syrup and thick gravy.

They sat on top of a brick wall that circled a tree, and Brent eagerly wolfed down his food. Philomela chewed hers more daintily, savoring the weird mix of additives. Above her chewing sounds, she heard a woman speak the fatal word to a companion.

"Murder. You know about the recent one of course."

"Yes. I wonder who did it."

Philomela stopped chewing and glanced around at the other side of the circular wall where a casually dressed couple sat and munched on salmon burgers. Looking straight ahead again, she surreptitiously listened to their verbal attempts to explain the horrendous incident.

"Melvin Springer could have done it," the woman said. "I understand Kathy Holmes jilted him several weeks ago."

Philomela's ears perked up as the man admitted to having heard that same bit of gossip. "Do you think he did her in?'

"I don't know. But having a wife murdered and now a girlfriend, it makes you wonder."

"Are you implying he did both of them in? Sort of like a Bluebeard?"

Philomela vaguely recalled the story of Bluebeard, a man who killed his numerous wives and inherited their worldly goods. He was more or less the male counterpart of a female Black Widow who killed her many husbands for their worldly goods. In both stories the motive for murder was greed—and in both stories the murderers succeeded in inheriting great wealth. However, their enjoyment of ill-gotten wealth was short lived because they both ended up being caught and paying for their misdeeds.

Philomela did not think Melvin fit the Bluebeard persona. She was tempted to turn around and explain to the couple that he had been cleared of any involvement with the death of his wife. However, if she offered the explanation, she would also admit to being an ordinary snoop.

The man and woman wandered away and Philomela continued eating her weird hotdog. Ruminating on the couple's conversation and their suspicion that Melvin Springer might be involved with Kathy's death, she recalled the two women in the History Café. They had implicated Tom Trust in Kathy's death. And what about the couple whose words she had overheard at lunch in the

Yacht Club? Like the couple just now, they, too, had suspected Melvin.

Tom Trust and Melvin Springer. Was it all mere gossip?

CHAPTER 12

Monday Morning.

Philomela and Brent entered the office of Trust Realty and the attractive young woman sitting at the front desk stood up, smiled, and said, "Good morning."

"Good morning, Annette." Philomela remembered briefly chatting with her when they had entered the office with Roger Thistle. "Any news about Kathy?"

Annette shook her head and her eyes grew moist. "She was my business mentor. She was always nice to me and very helpful."

"She was pleasant to us, too," Philomela said. "The day before her death, we spent the afternoon with her. I really enjoyed her sense of humor."

"If Roger hadn't made the previous arrangement with you two, I would have volunteered to become your realtor."

"Pardon?" Philomela was about to correct her regarding Roger having made a previous arrangement with them, but at that moment her flow of thoughts was interrupted by the man in question.

"Hello, Philomela and Brent." Roger strode past Annette's desk and shook the newcomers' hands. "Nice to see you again. Did you go to the market on Friday night?"

"We did," Philomela replied. "It had everything." She told him about their hotdogs.

"I don't know about that Canadian one. A mix of syrup and gravy doesn't turn me on." Then he voiced their reason for being in the office. "You're in luck today. A couple of new listings have appeared. They might fit your needs."

On his computer monitor he brought up virtual tours of two houses. Philomela noted the price. Though below the prices of the other houses he had shown them, they were still quite costly.

"The price is a bit less than what we've been looking at," she said. "Is something wrong with them?"

"Nothing's wrong with them. One is small and the other needs a lot of tender loving care. I have another house here, but it also needs a lot of work. They're not far from the office. Why don't I take you in my car? You can leave your truck here."

They proceeded toward the door, and Philomela smiled at Annette who was chatting with two new clients. She returned the smile, waved, and again paid attention to the couple sitting across the desk from her.

In the backseat of Roger's car, Philomela crossed her legs and watched the scenery pass by the window. Liking what she saw, she felt a flutter in her abdomen. If it hadn't been for Procne moving here, she and Brent would never have known about this delightful town. They would never have seen Main Avenue with its shops and history museum, nor would they have known about the flat terrain that's good for walking. Saltaire was a perfect place to retire.

The first house they viewed was cute and colorful but incredibly small. If she and Brent lived in it they would spend most of their time tripping over each other. In Philomela's mind it was overpriced. The second house had an almost perfect floor plan but the hardwood floors needed to be re-sanded, new carpets needed to be laid, and a toilet and a sink needed to be replaced. She figured the kitchen would be adequate if the cupboards were painted inside and out. She wondered what else needed to be done. Electrical wiring? Insulation? Plumbing? The third house was similar in plan to the second but it needed even more work—kitchen revamped, bathrooms upgraded and who knew about the wiring and plumbing? Outside in the garden she recognized rhododendrons and hydrangeas struggling to survive amongst the weeds.

"The owner was a widower who for a long time had poor health," Roger said. "During his later years, he didn't maintain the property very well and it was completely unattended when he went into a nursing home. It came on the market yesterday."

"Didn't he have any family to care for things?" Philomela asked.

"He had a son in Toronto who seldom got here. Obviously he paid little attention to the house and garden."

Roger then took them up a twisty, overgrown driveway to a house that was little more than a shack.

Philomela frowned. "Look at the pale, yellow paint. It's all peeling. There are two broken windows covered with plywood. The front steps sag dangerously." She asked the price and discovered it was well within their range.

"This place has been on the market for over a year," Roger said. "The land is nice for someone who wants to build a new house. This shack is a tear-down."

"It sure is," Brent said. "It should be blown up. But we're not interested in building a new house."

"There's no point in going inside," Philomela said.

Brent agreed and looked at his wristwatch.

"I have another commitment," Roger said, "so I apologize for not taking you out for lunch."

"It's just as well," Brent said. "Philomela and I need time to discuss what we've seen today. We have to decide if we want to renovate or wait for a house that needs little or no work."

CHAPTER 13

Monday Noon

After Roger dropped them off at the Seaside Motel, Philomela asked, "Where shall we go for lunch, Brent? The History Café?"

"Fine with me," Brent replied. "Its food seems consistently good. And the prices are reasonable."

"And," Philomela added, "Jean may have news about Kathy's death."

Brent gazed at his wife's face. "That's the main reason you want to go there, isn't it?"

"Not the main one, Brent. Just one of three reasons—good food, inexpensive prices, accurate and up-to-date news."

Inside the café they gave their orders to Jean then listened to her monologue about recent events. Unlike the gossip Philomela had overheard in the Yacht Club, here in the History Café, and at the street market, Jean focused on factual information.

"The police were here this morning," she said. "Constable James told me they found interesting fingerprints inside the crime scene. They're trying to match them to known offenders. The yellow tape is gone now, so the house will soon be on the market again. You should get your realtor to show it to you. I understand it is quite lovely. Because of what happened there, the owners have lowered the price. They just want to get rid of the place. It will be a good buy for someone."

Philomela and Brent listened quietly then carried their orders to a table for two and sat down. As Philomela munched her garden salad, she wondered about the crime scene. Could she cope with living in a place where someone had recently been murdered? Especially when the victim was someone she liked and had recently spent a few hours with? She knew her sensitivity to weather changes and the ambience of immediate surroundings would make living in such a house difficult, probably impossible. She asked Brent if he could live in such a place.

He shook his head and admitted, "It would take great willpower. I would need a long time period before I could stop thinking about the tragic happening."

"So," she asked, "should we ask Roger about seeing it?"

"It wouldn't hurt to look." He took a bite of his ham sandwich.

After lunch they walked to the real estate office. Roger wasn't there, so Brent asked Annette Murphy if she could show them the infamous house.

"Sure. I have two hours to spare before seeing my next client. I'll drive you in my Honda Civic."

Inside the former crime scene, Philomela found the house plan pleasing and the finishing very professional. The price Annette quoted was also pleasing—because the owner had dropped the price to within their range.

"I understand Kathy was killed between the living room and dining room," Philomela said.

"That's right." Annette stepped into the living room and pointed to an archway separating the two rooms.

Philomela glanced around the living room. When she had peered in the window, she could not see the body lying on the floor, only a shoe. She shuddered. If she hadn't enjoyed their time with Kathy, could she manage to live here? Doubtful. But as things were, it would be impossible to forget the girl's image. She shifted her feet and her eyes dropped along the wall to the floor. A tiny brown stain had been missed when the room was cleaned. Blood perhaps? She knew that photographs and fingerprints had been taken. Seeing a tiny piece of blue fabric stuck to the baseboard she bent down and pulled it free. With little thought she stuffed it in the pocket of her light jacket.

Annette suggested they go upstairs. Brent walked behind her and Philomela trailed behind. With each step she knew for sure she could never live in this house. Her empathy and sensitivities would not allow her to tolerate the ambience of horror and violence that permeated the entire place. It was as if the walls and floor had absorbed emotions of puzzlement, fear, pain, and anger. Puzzlement, fear and pain from the victim and anger from the perpetrator.

Why, she wondered, had the perpetrator been so angry with Kathy?

Outside, walking to the Honda Civic, Philomela thanked Annette for showing them the house and expressed why she couldn't live there.

"I understand," Annette said. "I feel the same way."

"We're considering two houses Roger showed us this morning," Philomela said, stopping beside the car. "But they aren't quite what we want. And they cost more than we should pay."

"I have another house with a large garage that might

be worth looking at. It's been on the market for eleven months and yesterday the price was reduced for the second time. But I'll warn you…a widow died and her adult children have been too busy to clean it."

"Let's go," Brent said.

Philomela smiled to herself—the house would have to be very dirty before Brent would even notice.

Annette parked her Honda in front of a bungalow situated across the street from houses bordering the ocean. Philomela was taken with the location. Why hadn't this place sold? Was the ambience bad? Had a murder been committed here?

Inside the house, she saw shoe-marks on the dusty floor, dirty windows that blocked the sun, two end tables that had seen better days, a broken dining room chair, two dirty glasses sitting beside the kitchen sink, five mismatched plates in an upper cupboard, old pots and pans inside a lower one, a single mattress on a bedroom floor, and a couple of dresses hanging in a closet. In an effort to enhance the basement, a bedroom and attached bathroom had been painted pale pink. Shelves lining the main part of the basement contained glass jars, magazines, and books that had been chewed by something.

Probably rats. Philomela shuddered. Apparently the widow's adult children couldn't overcome their grief long enough to clean or even tidy the place before putting it on the market. The first impression of careless disuse must have turned off many potential buyers, and possibly even some realtors. Dirt and clutter notwithstanding, the ambience in every room was pleasant. Philomela guessed the widow who lived here must, for the most part, enjoyed life. In fact, that could explain the children's lack of energy to clean. The loss of such a parent might have paralyzed them with grief.

Back at the real estate office, Annette subtly left them

on their own, allowing them space and time to freely discuss various ideas and options. Philomela spoke first.

"The junk needs to be removed, the house needs a good cleaning, and the yard needs work, but these things are doable. Everything on one floor is a bonus for people like us who are sneaking beyond middle age. The finished room in the basement could double as an office and spare bedroom."

Brent nodded. "Yes, a bungalow would be good, even though we aren't arthritic yet. However, it doesn't have a three-car garage."

"It has a big two-car garage with a small workshop at one end," Philomela said optimistically.

"What do you think? Do you like the place?" Brent asked.

"I like everything about it, except the junk and the dust motes. What about you?"

"Well, I could live with the two-car garage and workshop. And I like the location. The price is good. Should we make an offer?"

She nodded.

"I'll offer a couple of thousand less than what they're asking. That will more than covers cleaning costs."

"Especially if we do the work ourselves." With a grin Philomela added, "We might need a dumpster."

They walked over to Annette's desk and Brent told her about their prospective offer.

"That sounds reasonable. I'll phone the owners right away. If they agree shall I prepare the documents?"

"The final price will be subject to having a few basic checks done—roof, plumbing, electrical, foundation." Brent looked at his wife. "You're sure about this?"

She nodded. Then she raised her shoulders in a long shrug. "Are we crazy? Making a decision so quickly?"

"We both like the location and we see potential for the house. Besides, the price is right. If the house is basically sound and passes inspections, what more do we need?"

Philomela turned to the realtor. "Will Roger be annoyed that you made the sale, Annette?"

"He'll be disappointed. He should be annoyed with himself for neglecting to show it to you. It was on the market for eleven months."

"Yes, he had ample opportunity to show it to us," Philomela said. "It was an oversight on his part. He must have known the house is the size and price we requested."

Annette nodded and moved the conversation forward. "If the owners agree, I'll make arrangements to have the inspections done. Is there anything else you want to consider?"

"I don't think so," Brent said. "Just contact the people you normally use for such examinations. We should be aware if any major repairs are necessary. We don't want any surprises."

CHAPTER 14

Monday Afternoon

Noise pollution. Stop the noise pollution." The loud words startled Philomela. She stared at a man standing on a chair outside the History Café. Attired in what looked like a neon bicycle outfit, he waved his arms at passing vehicles. A truck roared past and he shook his fist angrily and yelled, "Stop the noise pollution."

Brent took Philomela's arm and guided her past the yelling man. At the door of the History Café, they both turned back, gave him a lingering look then went inside.

"Hi, you two," Jean said. "Is the Noise Pollution expert still creating noise out there?"

"He certainly is," Brent replied. "He causes more noise than all the pedestrians and big delivery trucks combined."

"He's a nuisance. How is your house hunting going?"

"Good." Philomela grinned like a cat that had caught a rat. "We found a house that suits us. So we've made an offer."

"Really? That didn't take long. I hope you'll soon become one of my regulars."

"Yes, we will." Philomela's grin widened and she ordered two small, regular coffees. While she waited for them, Brent sauntered over to one of two empty tables and sat down. Philomela thanked Jean, paid for the coffees, and carried them to where Brent was sitting. She set both mugs on the table and sat down across from him.

Brent said, "Our initial reaction to that house was exactly the same." He picked up his mug and took a tiny sip.

"Not only was our initial reaction the same, but so was our later analysis. We stayed on the same wavelength the whole time."

"Great minds think alike," Brent replied.

Philomela nodded and didn't voice the other half of the cliché—fools seldom differ.

"Fools or not, I think we made the right decision." Brent took another sip of coffee.

"I agree. I love everything about the house except the mess. If it had been cleaned up and perhaps staged, I bet it would have sold sooner and for a higher price."

"No doubt about it." Brent stared pensively at his coffee mug then raised his eyes to hers. "I wonder why Roger didn't show it to us. It fit all our parameters."

"He may have forgotten about it because it's been on the market for a long time. Or perhaps he just wanted to sell us a larger, costlier house."

"You mean he hoped to earn a bigger commission."

"It's possible," she said.

"The three houses he showed us this morning made me think there were no decent, realistically priced houses in this whole area."

"Well, thanks to Annette we saw two nice houses that were within our price range. And we actually chose one. When we finish our coffee, let's pop into Whimsical Woman and tell Procne our good news."

"We haven't bought it, yet," Brent reminded her.

"But we will."

"Is that what your gut feeling tells you?

She laughed and drank some of her caffeinated brew.

They finished their coffee and went outside. The pollution warrior now stood on a chair and pontificated about noisy airplanes. As they walked away, he switched his diatribe from noise pollution to global warming.

When Brent and Philomela entered Whimsical Woman, Procne glanced up from the cash counter, nodded, and completed the payment transaction with a customer. She placed the customer's purchase in a rusty orange bag and wished her a good day. As the customer sashayed to the door, Procne walked around the counter. "From the looks of you two, you've had a good day."

"We have, indeed." Philomela's grin broadened. "We made an offer on a house. But it hasn't been accepted...yet. It's part of an estate, and the family has paid little heed to cleaning up the house and yard. Annette said the owner was a widow who died eleven months ago."

"The realtor? Annette Murphy?"

"Yes. Do you know her?"

Procne nodded. "She's young and energetic. I've been told she's very conscientious."

"Roger wasn't at the office so Annette took us to see the crime-scene house. The yellow police tape had been removed. Brent and I knew we couldn't live in it. Annette then took us to the one that appealed to us. It's an untidy mess, but it's well constructed, has a good floor plan, and is in a nice location. It's across the street from the sea. Actually, it's not too far from the marina."

"Oh, I think I know the house you mean. I met the owner a couple of times. A nice old lady. She had cancer and it spread quickly. That's what happens in a retirement community. Real estate changes hands frequently. People retire to a house, move to a condo, then to an assisted living place, and finally to a care home where they die. Then new people retire to a house, move to a condo, etc., etc."

"The cycle of life in the seaside town of Saltaire."

"Dead on," Procne said.

Philomela ignored her pun. "Why don't the three of us have dinner at the Fireside Pizza this evening? Even though it's not a done deal, you can give us the scoop of the neighborhood. We'll really celebrate after the deal is done."

"I don't know anything about the neighborhood except what I've seen driving by." Then Procne added, "But at least no one was murdered in that house."

CHAPTER 15

Thursday Morning

Their prospective house passed the inspection checks faster and better than Philomela expected. The widow had had the roof replaced three years ago so the roof inspector said it should last another twenty years. The foundation was fine, but rats were a problem. A small hole in the basement was closed in hope of removing the creatures' access to the house, and traps and poison were spread around to reduce the population of those already inside.

Early Thursday morning, Brent and Philomela eagerly went to the office of Trust Realty. Happy with the inspections, they signed the papers to finalize the deal. They also were happy that the house was empty and that the widow's children were eager to settle the estate. Brent and Philomela were given immediate occupancy. As Annette handed Brent the keys to the house, Philomela saw Roger enter the office.

"Good morning, Roger," she said as he strode past her. With not so much as a nod of the head, he disappeared into his inner office. "Good grief, Brent, we're in his bad books. Should we apologize for using another realtor?"

"He should apologize to us," Brent replied. "He should have shown us that house on our first day with him."

Philomela looked over at Annette who was shaking her head. "He's probably angry because we realtors all agreed that the seller of Kathy's listings would also get her listing commission. Kathy had listed the house you just purchased."

"So, you get both the listing and the selling commissions," Brent said.

"Yes, but…"

"No buts," Brent interrupted. "You deserve it. Roger had his chance to do the same. You showed us the house, you took us to see it a second time, you arranged to have things checked, and you also helped eliminate the unwanted guests in the basement. You did all the paperwork and more. Now the deal is done. Done without a hitch."

Annette flushed slightly. "You make me sound better than I am."

At that point, Roger entered the room again. This time he sauntered toward the threesome.

"Roger," Philomela said. "Sorry you didn't find the right house for us."

Roger didn't reply. After a brief silence, Brent filled the vacuum. "Annette showed us one that fit all our requirements. So we made the deal."

"Which house is it?" Roger glared at Annette and she told him. "Yes. I remember it as being a terrible mess."

"But worth cleaning up," Philomela said. She was pleased that Roger no longer seemed overly angry. She suspected he realized he could blame no one but himself for missing the sale. She held the house keys up in the air. "Now we'll go to the hardware store and buy cleaning equipment. For the next couple of days our work will be cut out for us."

They ended up buying a vacuum cleaner, a broom, a dustpan, a mop with rectangular bucket, and cloths for dusting and washing. Brent found a window scraper with a long handle and added it to the things to be purchased. Philomela included detergent and another liquid cleaner. They hadn't ordered a dumpster so she picked up a box of large green garbage bags.

As Brent parked the truck in the driveway of their new abode, Philomela gazed at it contentedly. "This is our Mount Olympus. You and I, the god and goddess, will dwell within it forever. We'll feast on ambrosia and nectar and abide in perfect blessedness. As Homer said, *no wind will shake the untroubled peace.*"

"Sounds great. Shall I make a big sign?"

"Not until Olympus is cleared of clutter and carefully cleaned—inside and out."

So, that's what they did. First, they cleared out large unwanted stuff from both the main floor and the basement and set them near the curb for pick up—either by sanitation engineers or by seekers of discarded treasures. In the newly cleared basement Philomela saw a huge rat staring at her. She froze. Then she screamed. Brent rushed downstairs but her screams had encouraged the creature to hide so he missed seeing it.

"I guess that unwanted guest was too smart to take poison or get caught in a rat trap," he said.

Into large green garbage bags they dumped bottles, cans, and all the old magazines and books whose glue had provided dinner for the rodents. From the appearance of the books it was obvious that glue had been a favorite treat. Brent went upstairs to wash windows and she vacuumed and dusted the basement. Then she did the same on the main floor.

He went off to Starbucks for two medium sized coffees. When he returned, they sat on the front step, sipped the energizing coffee and wallowed in sunshine. After their brief break, she washed cupboards inside and out, Brent completed the window cleaning then helped scrub floors and walls. By four in the afternoon they were finished.

"Done." Philomela looked around, feeling tired but satisfied. "We can buy a bed and sleep here tonight."

"I don't think so. We'll need more than just a bed. Tomorrow we'll buy several basics and check out of our motel."

"How can I argue with an engineer's logic?" Actually, she appreciated the way his mind worked, calculating things in chronological order. Her mind, she had to admit, didn't always do that.

As Brent locked the front door, Philomela saw a white-haired lady hurrying across the lawn toward them.

"Hello," she said. "I'm so happy you bought the house. The former owner and I were lifelong friends. I'm Mary Skidmore, just call me Mary." She held out her gnarled right hand.

Philomela took hold of it gently, fearing she might injure the skin and bones of the fragile fingers. "I'm pleased to meet you, Mary. I'm Philomela and this is my husband, Brent Lark."

Mary smiled at Brent. "Thank goodness the house finally sold. I'm afraid the kids didn't understand much about marketing. They were very good to their mother, visiting at every opportunity. But after she died, they neglected the house and yard. Oh well, that's water under the bridge now. Do you like to garden?"

"We've never gardened on the west coast," Philomela said. "I know it's quite different from gardening under the Chinook Arch, on the prairies, and in the mountains."

Mary looked puzzled so Philomela explained, "The westerly Chinook winds climb over the Rocky Mountains and create mild weather in the middle of winter. Only hardy trees and plants can survive the frequent thawing and freezing."

Mary laughed. "I have heard of them. Out here, of course, we garden eleven months of the year, not three or four months like the rest of Canada. When you're settled, I'll help you identify trees and plants."

"I'll appreciate that," Philomela said. "I know spruce, pine, birch and poplar trees. And that's about it."

"That's a good start. You have an Arbutus tree and a fig tree in the back yard."

"I know the Arbutus, though I hadn't noticed it. It's such a striking tree, especially when losing its bark."

"Yes, they're busy trees—they lose flowers, berries, and bark. In the summer they're unwelcome near patios and decks because they drop prickly leaves."

"I have to confess I don't know fig trees."

"You soon will. All in good time."

"Mary, you've lived next door for a long time then."

"About forty years. I'm an old, nurse. I retired from the local hospital twenty-eight years ago."

Philomela studied Mary's face and figure. The lines on her face were minimal and her body held little excess fat. "You must have retired at age thirty."

Mary laughed. "No, I retired at age sixty. I would have worked longer, but my husband developed lung cancer so I stayed home and looked after him."

Philomela opened her mouth to ask if her husband survived and then thought better of it. She didn't want to be overly snoopy.

"My husband," Mary said, answering Philomela's un-asked question, "had chemo. He lived another year then got pneumonia and died."

"Oh, I'm sorry."

"I missed him terribly. For that matter, I still miss him. But life goes on." She smiled and spread her arms. "I have my garden and children and grandchildren. Nursing has changed so much that I'm afraid I've been left in the dust. However, new treatments for illnesses still interest me."

"Doubtless the basics of patient care are the same."

"A lot of that has changed, too. Now, after surgery, patients are encouraged to be ambulatory almost immediately. No more complete bed rest. In olden times, bed sores were hopefully prevented with back rubs. Now, bed sores and back rubs are things of the past."

Philomela wondered about Mary Skidmore's age. Too polite to ask, she mentally calculated—Mary retired twenty-eight years ago at age sixty. That would make her...eighty-eight. "Good grief," she blurted. "How do you keep looking so young?"

Mary laughed gaily. "Not that young. I keep active and eat a lot of fresh, nourishing produce."

"So, you believe in the adage that we are what we eat?"

"Without question. Hippocrates, almost three thousand years ago, said, 'Let food be thy medicine and medicine thy food.' He knew what he was talking about."

"I think I could learn a lot from you."

Mary laughed again, and Philomela thought of another old adage—Laughter is the best medicine.

"Well, I must go. I'm meeting a friend for an early dinner at the History Café."

Watching her walk briskly to her front door and disappear inside her house, Philomela mused on the things she would learn about retirement in Saltaire. Gardening and nutrition for starters.

Then her mind jumped from the sprightly octogenarian to two other women. The contrasts were sharp.

One woman had been prematurely laid to rest and the other, in middle age, barely existed. The first died from the murderous hands of another, and the second survived because of the kindly care of others.

CHAPTER 16

Thursday Evening

Philomela and Brent dressed for a celebratory dinner in the Saltaire Hotel dining room. They knew it was a classier place than the Fireside Pizza, so they discarded their grubby clothes and put on what local residents would describe as "smart casual." Philomela donned her brown Fantastic Frock—the dress that always traveled with her and always came out of the suitcase looking unwrinkled and attractive. Brent wore khaki pants that showed off his slim hips and a white shirt that accentuated his tanned skin.

They arrived at the dining room before Procne did. The hostess seated them at a table near a window overlooking a wide patio and a green lawn that extended to the Pacific Ocean. Philomela had learned this part of the ocean was locally known by its' indigenous name—Salish Sea. A waitress appeared and Brent ordered a bottle of champagne. The waitress set it on the table just as Procne arrived.

"Wow," she said. "Champagne. You should purchase a house more often."

Brent stood up and held out a chair for her. She thanked him and sat down. He returned to his chair and all three watched the waitress pop the cork, pour the champagne into three flute glasses, and then depart.

Philomela picked up her glass and held it toward her dinner companions. "I want to propose a toast to Olympus."

"Olympus?" Procne's eyebrows arched and her eyes looked questioningly at her sister.

"That's the name we've given our new abode. Mount Olympus, as you well know, is the home of gods and goddesses in Greek mythology."

"I don't believe your house is on a hill, let alone on a mountain."

"It's on a slight rise of land—about three inches." Brent chuckled and explained, "That's why we call it Olympus, not Mount Olympus."

"And you two are the god and goddess who dwell there." Procne's eyes sparkled as if reflecting the Champagne.

"Correct." Philomela laughed.

They clinked glasses and sipped the bubbly.

Brent smacked his lips. "I prefer beer, but this is okay for a special occasion."

"Nectar of the gods," Procne said.

"Actually," Philomela said, "I prefer a dry white wine. But I agree, this is good for a special occasion."

Over dinner, the new homeowners related anecdotes about what had happened during the last few days. Brent bragged about washing windows and Philomela described the rat in the basement.

Procne responded with a "Good on you" for the windows and a "Yuk" for the rats and continued eating. She later described the arrival and unpacking of a box of new clothes from a wholesaler and concluded by saying, "The coats and jackets are not only practical but lovely. Phil-omela, a couple of them would look smashing on you."

"I'll come by tomorrow or the next day, after we buy a bed and move into Olympus. Once we're permanent resi-dents in Saltaire, I'll try and be more fashionable. I don't want to embarrass my trendy kid sister."

"All you have to do is fork over a couple of small bucks."

Philomela chuckled. "You mean a few big bills."

Their conversation ebbed as a flurry of excitement caught their interest. Four newcomers sat down at a table adjacent to them and they were abuzz with news.

One of the male newcomers leaned toward Brent. "Have you heard?"

"Heard what?" Brent asked.

"There's been another murder."

Brent stared at him. "Another person killed? Here? In Saltaire?"

"This town is becoming downright dangerous," the man said.

"Good grief." Philomela placed both hands at each side of her face. "Who was the victim?"

"We don't know," a lady interjected. "I'm just glad it wasn't me or my friend."

Philomela no longer felt like celebrating. It seemed a serial killer lived in their new hometown.

CHAPTER 17

Friday Morning

Intending to break their fast at the History Café, Brent and Philomela walked from the Seaside Motel. The eastern sun beamed on their backs and the soft moist air enveloped them. Last evening's startling news was in abeyance, so everything seemed right with the world.

Inside the café, Brent hurried to a table being vacated by three people. Philomela walked up to the food counter, greeted Jean Greenfield and asked for two coffees and two senior breakfast specials—each advertising one egg, two slices of bacon, fruit or hash-brown potatoes, and one slice of toast. Philomela knew from the café owner's expression that she knew everything wasn't right with the world—at least not in the town of Saltaire.

"For the past few days the talk of the town has been a murder," Jean said. "Now it's two murders."

"At dinner last night fellow diners told us about the second murder. But no one knew any details."

"A new name has been added to the death of Kathy Holmes. It's terribly disconcerting." Leaning on the counter, Jean seemed ready to burst into tears.

"Do you know who the latest victim is?" Philomela hoped the victim wasn't a relative of Jean's.

"Annette Murphy."

"Good grief!" Philomela felt faint. Her left hand fluttered to her heart and her right hand clutched the counter. "Both victims were realtors. Both had helped Brent and me search for the perfect house." She took a deep breath. "Roger Thistle—he helped us, too. Will he be the next victim?"

"Do you think they were killed because they were realtors?" Jean asked. "Or because they were women?"

"I have no idea. Do you know how it happened?"

"The same as before. Like Kathy, Annette was supposed to show a house to clients, a husband and wife. Unlike before, she supposedly had met them the day before at the office, so it seemed perfectly safe."

"How was she killed?"

"Strangled," Jean replied.

Philomela had trouble forming any words. "Kathy's death…is hard to understand…but…but Annette's is even harder. Why would anyone murder a young, innocent girl just launching her career?"

Jean answered with a shrug. Her hand was unsteady as she poured coffee into two mugs. "I've known Annette for years. She was a quiet, hard working girl. Not a mean bone in her body." Jean set the full coffee mugs on the counter and gazed at Philomela. "Who will be murdered next?"

"Hopefully no one will." Philomela looked pensively at the owner of the café. "Strangulation takes strength…the murderer is probably a man. Though I must admit some women are incredibly strong." She sighed loudly.

"Constable James and Corporal Stinson are here having coffee right now." Jean glanced toward the table where the police sat. "They've been asking questions. But they haven't given any hint as to who the killer might be."

"They probably don't know. Did they say where Annette's body was found?"

"Inside the house she was apparently showing. The owners were away for three days. They returned late yesterday afternoon and found the body. Constable James said the medical examiner determined Annette had been killed early Thursday afternoon."

Thursday afternoon, Philomela thought. She and Brent had finalized their house deal with Annette Thursday morning. What good would her double commission be to her now?

She carried the coffee mugs over to Brent, set them on the table, and sat down. She related the information Jean had just imparted.

For a moment Brent was speechless. Then he asked, "Do you think this town is jinxed?"

"Almost looks like it. This is a dreadful situation. I feel sick. I can't believe that within the last week two people we were dealing with have been murdered. It's horrible." Philomela wondered if Brent now understood how she sometimes got caught up in helping to solve murders.

As if reading her mind, he looked at her sternly, "There's nothing we can do, Philomela."

"You're right. We should simply steer clear and let the police do their job."

"Definitely. Please remember to practice what you preach."

Well, she thought, he still doesn't fully understand my involvement is such things. "Brent, if the opportunity arises, how can I not help the police?"

As she finished speaking Corporal Stinson walked near their table and Constable James followed close on his heels.

Philomela couldn't help herself. "Constable James," she said, and the policewoman stopped and looked at her. "I'm Philomela Nightingale, Procne Ellis's sister." She lowered her voice, not wanting everyone in the café to hear her words. "We met during your investigation of Maxine Springer's murder."

"Of course. I remember. Nice to see you again."

"My husband Brent and I just bought a house in Saltaire. Kathy Holmes and Annette Murphy were our realtors. Annette helped us close the deal yesterday morning." Philomela saw the constable's eyes widen.

"Did Annette seem worried about anything?" Constable James asked.

"No. Quite the contrary. She seemed very happy, especially about making the sale. I'm sure she didn't suspect anything was wrong anywhere. Do you think she was targeted? Or did she happen to be at the wrong place at the wrong time?"

"We don't know." The constable took a business card from her pocket and handed it to Philomela. "You may have been one of the last people to see her alive. If something comes to mind, no matter how inconsequential, please give me a call."

"I will." Philomela took the card and dropped it in her purse.

"If necessary, how can I contact you?"

Philomela dug in her purse and brought out her own business card. "We don't have a landline yet, but here's my cell number. I don't always have it turned on. Perhaps I should give you our new address."

"That might be helpful."

Philomela wrote the address of their new home on the back of the card and handed it to the constable. Then she watched the policewoman walk to the front of the café and follow her coworker out the door.

Brent groaned. "Philomela, you're doing it again."

She tried to look innocent. "Doing what again?"

"Getting involved with a murder case."

"Well...not really."

"Yes, really. The murderer might find out you're talking to police and begin stalking you."

"I don't think so. I just want Constable James to know we had seen Annette on the day she was killed. It's unlikely we'll be able to help...but you never know. And you have to admit, you want the killer brought to justice as much as I do."

"I admit that. But I don't want you to be at risk. Please let the police to their job." He drained his coffee mug.

A waitress came by and refilled both their mugs. A few minutes later she brought their senior breakfasts and set them on the table.

"After we check out of the motel, should we take our suitcases to Olympus before we go shopping?" Philomela tried to behave in a positive manner.

"I think we should. That'll leave more room in the truck for all our new purchases."

Thinking of what they must buy, she did her utmost to push the two murders to the back of her mind.

CHAPTER 18

Friday Morning, Later

In spite of all the tragic news about their realtors, Philomela and Brent managed to enjoy shopping. First, they purchased a king size bed. It would be delivered later that afternoon which would allow them to christen it that evening. Second, at the same store, they bought sheets, pillows, pillow cases, a duvet, and duvet cover. They didn't plan to buy any more bedroom furniture until they moved in and could see exactly what they needed. Third, they went to the dollar store and bought two plates, two mugs, two knives, and two forks.

At the hardware store they purchased a small pot, a small frying pan, and a small coffee pot. At a bathroom store they bought two bath towels, two facecloths, and a set of kitchen dish cloths and tea towels. The truck was well packed when they added a few basic food items from a local grocery store.

Placing a bag of fresh produce in the back of the vehicle, Philomela said, "The truck is a good grocery-getter."

"Do we have enough food to last a few days?"

"Who knows?"

Brent gazed at her pensively. "When do you want to make the life-changing move?"

"Well, Janice and Frank need to give a month's notice on their apartment. They're eager to settle into our old abode, so they'll start things in motion the instant we give the word. I'll email her as soon as we book a moving company."

"I ask again. Philomela, when do you want to make the actual move?"

A lump in her throat prevented her from immediately answering. Unexpectedly, she was experiencing mixed emotions about leaving their cozy nest situated on the floor above the office of her magazine. Their small upstairs home had been comfortable for both of them and very convenient for her. She had been happy there.

But she liked the town of Saltaire and their newly purchased house. She expected to be happy here, too. Provided the serial murderer was soon apprehended.

She swallowed the lump in her throat and climbed into the passenger side of the truck. "To answer your question, Brent, maybe we could move in four weeks."

"That would be good for me. I have commitments in the next three weeks, but after that I'll be able to find time to help with the move."

"Good."

Initially, Philomela had dragged her feet about selling her business and moving to the Pacific Northwest. For more than twelve years she had spent most of her waking hours interviewing, writing, assembling, editing and publishing her baby—"The Integrator." However, last month she figuratively hung up her computer and allowed her employee to more or less act as editor and publisher. Though she knew Janice would do a good job, she had been reluctant to hand over the keyboard for the final editing.

Over the years, compiling and publishing the magazine had been so much fun. She had met interesting people, written fascinating articles about them, and advertised local products and services. The magazine business was never overly lucrative, but it always earned enough to pay the bills and—she smiled at the thought—keep her in trendy shoes.

Soon the magazine would be out of her hands. Janice and her veterinarian husband had already made a good down payment on the business and the two-story house. So, in about four weeks, Philomela and Brent would move to this gentler climate and embark on a more leisurely lifestyle—retirement for her and semi-retirement for him.

Living in Saltaire as a retired person would be a drastic change. After getting settled in their new digs, how would she spend her time?

She could read the classics she meant to read during her student and working years but never had time to do so. She had managed to get through Tolstoy's *War and Peace* but not Gibbons' *Decline and Fall of the Roman Empire.* She wanted to reread Dostoevsky's *Crime and Punishment.* She could volunteer in some capacity—perhaps at the Adept Adult Day Centre. Would she be any good at dealing with seniors with health problems? Did she have the right personality to be a caregiver?

Doubtless she would relieve Procne at Whimsical Woman whenever her sister needed help. And that would be fun.

Perhaps she and Brent could adopt a dog or a cat. There were lots of dogs in Saltaire, and outside the door of almost every business sat a water dish for pets to hydrate themselves. She had noticed how dog owners carefully used plastic bags to religiously scoop the poo their pets deposited on sidewalks and lawns. That was important—she didn't want her shoes wrecked by dog feces, no matter how cute the pet might be.

Then, of course, there were the deaths of Kathy Holmes and Annette Murphy. At the moment there seemed nothing she could do to help solve either of their horrible deaths.

But a niggling thought wondered if her sleuthing skills would once again come to the fore. She honestly hoped so. The idea of the killer not being caught was beyond thinking about.

CHAPTER 19

Friday Afternoon and Evening

They ate a quick lunch at the Dairy Queen then drove to their new home. Brent parked the truck in the garage, and they lugged their purchases into Olympus. At one point, Philomela stopped and wondered about a house sign—should the words be bold print or fancy script? She mentally slapped herself for straying off the job at hand and continued carrying things into the house.

She rinsed their new kitchen utensils in the sink and dried them with a new dish towel. After putting the few glasses, plates, and mugs in a kitchen cupboard, Philomela realized they had no chairs or table.

"Brent, should we go to a secondhand store to get a small table and chairs?"

"There's no point buying stuff we won't need after our furniture arrives from Calgary. Perhaps Procne could lend us a couple of chairs."

"I have a better idea. We have no patio furniture in Calgary, so…"

He didn't wait for her to finish. "Excellent idea."

His prompt approval excited her. "We could keep the outside furniture in the living room until our furniture arrives from Calgary then move it out on the back patio."

"Once again, two great minds think alike."

Once again, she didn't add the last part of the cliché.

"The store gave us a two-hour window for delivery of the bed and bedding." Philomela was pensive for a several seconds then added, "We could plunk our buttocks on the front steps and enjoy a cup of afternoon water, or coffee. We have no tea."

"I should have bought a six pack of beer."

"Better still, we could unpack our suitcases and hang—oh, oh, no coat hangers."

She filled two glasses with water, took two small oranges from the fridge, and they carried them to the front steps and sat down.

It was four o'clock when two burly delivery men carried the bed into the master bedroom and efficiently helped Philomela and Brent set it up. After they left, Philomela opened up plastic packages and put bottom sheets on the bed. Then she stuffed new pillows into new pillowcases. With a bit more effort she stuffed the duvet inside the duvet cover.

"The temperature is comfortably warm," Brent said. "We won't need anything more than a top sheet."

Their food purchases had been mainly for breakfasts and lunches, so Philomela suggested they go someplace for dinner. They decided on a Chinese restaurant. Brent drove the truck on a scenic route along a tree lined street they had not traversed before.

Looking around, Philomela gasped. "Look, there's the yellow police tape. That must be the house where Annette was murdered."

Brent slowed the truck and they gawked at the house and yard. A lone man in uniform stood guard. The house was Tudor style with white stucco and brown beams. Flowering shrubs added dashes of color and a gently curving walk seemed to invite visitors to jump the yellow tape and walk to the house.

"We've been so busy this afternoon," Philomela said, "I'd almost forgotten about the two murders. I wonder if the police have any leads regarding the identity of the perpetrator."

"The sooner they find him the better." With a serious facial expression, he glanced at her. "Then you won't get involved."

She ignored his latter statement and focused on the first one. "You think the murderer is a man?"

He nodded. "Strangulation would require physical strength on the part of the strangler."

"You're right. Not many women could slay someone by choking them. Most women would have trouble holding a struggling person down until the victim's breathing ceased."

"Philomela, let's forget it and allow the police to solve the murders. They're capable and have lots of experience in such matters."

"Of course."

Though not their doing, the subject was not forgotten. It came up again inside the Chinese restaurant.

The hostess led them to a table adjacent to one occupied by two men. Philomela recognized Simon Fraser immediately. But it took a few minutes for her to realize the man hiding behind facial hair was Melvin Springer. She wondered if he had grown a mustache and beard in order to develop a new persona after becoming a widower a year and a half ago.

Casually overhearing part of their conversation, she surreptitiously listened to it more carefully. Like most people in town they were discussing the two murders.

Throughout the entire meal, Philomela tuned in and out of their conversation. Though they spoke softly, she heard them debate the reasons someone would choose certain weapons for murder.

"A rope could be used to strangle a person," Simon said.

"Or pantyhose." Melvin looked pensively at his dinner partner. "An axe or hammer would be too bloody and a gun would be too noisy. Poison would be difficult to administer."

"Getting back to strangulation. Not everyone is husky enough to hold a person down while stopping the breath of life. It's unlikely that a woman could do it."

"Lots of women could be strong enough to do the deed, especially if she was angry or jealous of the victim." Melvin cleared his throat, sipped his wine, and continued peaking, "Annette and Kathy were stylish, good looking, and successful. Lots of people, male and female, aren't born with so many attributes. Nor do they develop the drive and work ethic needed to succeed in their chosen jobs. Those who suffer from the green-eyed monster often say and do bad things."

Philomela peripherally saw Simon nod his head and heard him say, "Off hand, I can't think of anyone who would be that jealous of them."

"Oh, I can think of a couple of people," Melvin said, "but I won't mention any names because I don't want to spread rumors that are probably untrue."

"Being preoccupied with other things—Angelina's illness primarily—I haven't given the murderer any deep thought."

"Understandable. Is there any hope of a cure?"

"Not yet. But at least she still often knows me."

"I thought Maxine's death was the worst thing that could happen. But seeing what you and Angelina are going through, I'm no longer so sure."

"Both situations are bad. Different, but bad." Simon cleared his throat and looked down at his almost empty plate.

Philomela wondered if he was hiding tears. She looked across the table at Brent and saw that he, too, was listening to the neighboring conversation. He picked up a chunk of sweet and sour pork with his chopsticks and popped it in his mouth. Then he glanced over at her.

"Are you joining me as a snoop?" she asked.

"Not purposely. One thing I'm beginning to realize—you and I should enjoy life while we're still healthy."

"Well spoken. Perhaps we could do some traveling." For a few minutes she concentrated on wielding her chopsticks and savoring each bite of almond chicken. Then her neighbors' conversation again caught her attention.

"I understand you and Kathy Holmes dated a few times," Simon said.

"Yes," Melvin said. "We enjoyed a few social activities together. But before it got too serious, we parted company."

"Were you incompatible?"

"I guess so."

Philomela thought she detected a note of bitterness in Melvin's last statement. Was the incompatibility one-sided? If so, was it on Kathy's side or on Melvin's side?

"You'll find it difficult to replace Maxine," Simon said. "She was such an incredible woman. However, you're still relatively young and someone else may enter your life and help fill the void."

Melvin responded sotto voce. "Simon, I'm really not looking for another commitment. But Tom and Sheila Trust think I should be looking. They were the ones who first hooked me up with Kathy Holmes. After we split they tried twice more to hook me up with other young ladies. The two ladies were pleasant enough, but we had no mutual attraction. Neither of us had much desire to see each other again."

"Was one of the young lady's another of Tom's realtors?"

"One was a nurse Sheila had met in the dress shop. I liked the young woman, but our relationship was brief and platonic. We had very little in common."

Philomela wondered about the identity of the other young lady.

"I'm surprised Tom would go to the trouble of playing cupid," Simon said.

"Sheila probably did the organizing, trying to be a matchmaker. Tom's a pleasant fellow who simply enjoys having dinner with people who are interested in real estate."

Philomela gave her head a slight nod, surreptitiously agreeing with Melvin's assessment of Tom Trust. She knew he and Sheila were good neighbors to Procne, and Tom efficiently presided over the strata council. Procne and the other four strata members felt fortunate to have him as president—he knew what to look for, what to do, and handled surprise problems with ease. For the most part Sheila did what was necessary, but mostly she lived and breathed her work in Upscale Garments.

Because, a year and a half ago, Philomela had helped Sheila and Procne with their memorial fashion-show for Maxine Springer, she had gotten to know Sheila reasonably well. She certainly knew Sheila better than she knew Tom. But on the few occasions she had talked with Tom he always had been very pleasant.

Peripherally, she now saw Melvin and Simon quietly split and pay their dinner bill. Having come up with no real clues regarding the murders, they got up from the

table and left the restaurant. Neither had paid any attention to other diners. That didn't surprise Philomela because she knew both men were consumed with different
problems—one a recuperating widower and the other adjusting to his wife's early dementia. She suspected their
serious concerns often triggered clouds of depression. If
only she could be a fairy godmother, wave her magic
wand, and quickly remove any darkness floating around
their heads.

"Do you think it will take long to pack up our goods
and chattels in Calgary?" Brent asked.

"No. The hard part will be deciding what to sell and
give away. Once that is done, we can concentrate on
packing." She glanced out the window at a blue flowering shrub. "To inspire our packing, I'll think of that beautiful blue hydrangea."

"Will that truly be of any help?"

"Yes," she replied. "Conversely, I could think of leaving thirty below freezing weather and moving to a place
whose temperature seldom goes below freezing."

"But the cold there is dry and here the cold is damp."

She laughed. "That's a fallacy. Dry cold weather is
much the same as damp cold weather."

"No, it isn't. Damp is colder because it gets into the
bones."

"This conversation is getting ridiculous."

"Maybe. But it's better than rehashing the deaths of
the two young realtors."

Philomela nodded and gazed thoughtfully at her husband.

"It just crossed my mind…Melvin didn't tell Simon
the name of his second date that Tom had organized."

"Is that important?"

"It might be."

CHAPTER 20

Saturday Morning

The doorbell rang and Philomela hurriedly left the kitchen. Opening the front door of her new home, she was surprised to see Tom Trust standing on the top step.

"Good morning Philomela. I just popped by to see if everything regarding your house is okay."

"Everything's fine, Tom. Except, of course, Annette's death."

"Another terrible tragedy. My two best realtors gone. I hope the police soon find the killer. Or killers." He bit his lower lip and shook his head. "I tried to call you on your cellphone."

"Oh, I had it turned off."

"It doesn't matter. I was appraising a house nearby so decided to stop by. Normally, your realtor would check with you. Due to the unfortunate circumstances, I'm here to make sure all is well with you and Brent. I want our clients to be satisfied."

"I appreciate your concern, especially when you probably have lots of other things to do. Because of recent events, I'm sure your office is in turmoil."

"It's not its usual humming self. The new game is paranoia. Everyone in the office wonders if some nutcase is targeting realtors. As a result, we, including me, keep looking over our shoulders expecting to see a tie-wielding crazy coming after us."

"Tie-wielding?"

"The police just released that information. Both girls were strangled with a man's tie."

"That's awful. Do the police think the murderer is targeting realtors?"

"It looks that way."

For a few seconds Philomela hesitated. Then she asked, "Would you like to come in for coffee?"

"Thanks, but I must get back to the office. A million things to do."

"Annette thought of everything for us. We have no questions or complaints."

"Good. I'm going to miss her. In the meantime, if I can be of any help please let me know."

She watched him make a hundred and eighty degree turn and stroll down the walk to his white Cadillac. He nonchalantly looked over his shoulder and waved to her, as if free from worry. She suspected he was putting on a good act. Like everyone else in town, he worried about being targeted as the next victim. Realtors and females seemed the likely targets, but who knew for sure? The next victim could be anyone in the general population.

The only person with no concerns about being murdered would be the perpetrator. Surely that person couldn't be Tom Trust. Two gossiping women in the café had tried to superficially implicate him with murder. Philomela didn't hold their remarks in good stead. Tom didn't appear to be a psychopath or even a narcissist. And he was too good a businessman to purposely get rid of two capable employees. These points should immediately rule him out as the perpetrator.

Or should they? Prospective home buyers might feel sorry for him so out of sympathy give his real estate company their business. Like Jean Greenfield, he might thrive on the bad news.

Philomela's rumination was interrupted by Brent walking from the master bedroom into the kitchen. His hair was wet from a shower and he was buttoning his short-sleeved shirt. He smiled at her. "Who was at the door?"

"Tom Trust." She explained.

"That was decent of him. Especially since his business world must be in a terrible mess. Speaking of messes, what's on your agenda for today?"

"We could eat a makeshift breakfast of fruit and yo-ghurt or go out. I need to pick up a few more things at the grocery store. I promise to cook breakfast tomorrow—perhaps bacon and eggs."

"Good."

"Let's go to the History Café right now."

"To get the latest gossip from Jean?"

"Brent, you're too smart by far. But it's news I want, not gossip. Jean's news is based on fact, not on baseless rumor."

Inside the History Café, Brent made a beeline to the only empty table available. Philomela stood at the serving counter, smiled at Jean, and ordered two coffees and two full English breakfasts. Taking advantage of the owner's close proximity, she leaned on the counter and asked about the murders.

"The last news I heard," Jean said, "came from Melvin Springer while he enjoyed a coffee break. He left a few minutes ago. Yesterday he talked with Corporal Stinson who told him things were progressing. Apparently some fingerprints have provided the police with a prime suspect."

"They actually have a prime suspect?" Philomela was surprised.

"Apparently. But they don't have enough evidence to charge the person."

"Do you know who it is?" Philomela asked.

"No. According to Melvin, the corporal gave the impression it's someone we normally wouldn't suspect. A respected citizen."

"Good grief. That's worse than a drifter coming here on a killing spree."

"I know. Now I study each customer and ask myself, 'Is he or she the guilty person?' I even suspected Simon Fraser when he popped in for his regular latte."

"Did you tell him of your suspicions?"

"No."

"What about Tom Trust?"

"He hasn't been here recently. But he, too, would fit the description of a respected citizen."

"Have you heard that the girls were strangled with a man's tie?"

"No. Who told you that?"

"Tom Trust told me. This morning he came by to make sure we were happy with our new domicile." Jean frowned and Philomela added, "He mentioned that members of his staff are terribly paranoid—everyone thinks the murderer is specifically after people who work at Trust Realty."

"All his staff? Not just females?"

"That's what he said. He includes himself in that group. I hope the murderer's list doesn't include people who do or did business with Trust Realty."

"Oh, Philomela. How nerve-wracking for you and Brent. Do you worry about being the next victim?"

"Occasionally. Especially since both victims were females. What about you?"

Jean handed Philomela two steaming coffee mugs. "I'm female. I no longer go anyplace alone, especially at night."

CHAPTER 21

Saturday Morning, Continued

Side by side, Brent and Philomela sauntered along Main Avenue. Before reaching Brent's truck, a familiar voice called, "Philomela."

She turned and at first didn't recognize the woman dressed as if in mourning—black tight pants and black baggy sweater. As the caller drew near, Philomela realized the woman was the local psychic, looking anything but her usual airy-fairy self. Her unusual sartorial splendor resembled a black crow rather than a silver-blue dove.

"Selene, how nice to see you. I'd like you to meet my husband, Brent Lark." She explained to Brent that Selene Hamilton, Procne's friend and neighbor, had two beautiful cats. "The black one is called Hecate and the white one is called Artemis."

Brent grinned. "Nice to meet you, Selene. You'd better guard your cats. My wife's a cat lover. She may spirit them away."

"How would I do that?" Philomela suspected that Brent had no idea how close he had come to describing Selene's spiritual tendencies. His interests centered on science and reality, not on souls and spirits. When he answered her question by saying, "Entice them from Selene with catnip," she grinned then focused on the psychic. "Selene, we've just bought a house. Once we're settled, we'll have you over. I might even look for a cat, not yours of course. We have a few rats and our new next-door neighbor said the best way to get rid of rats is to get a cat. Besides, Brent hit the nail on the head. I do love cats."

"Appreciating cats is one more thing you and I have in common. Your new neighbor is right about rodents. Though we live next to the ocean, Hecate and Artemis keep our building rat free."

"No wonder. Your cats are above average in intelligence."

Selene chuckled but didn't disagree.

Leaving the subject of felines, Philomela said, "We're calling our new home, Olympus.*"*

Once again Selene chuckled. "My goodness, will all the gods and goddesses rally there? Just kidding. Right now I'm on my way to Whimsical Woman. Procne phoned about a customer whose new dress needs the waist taken in and the hemline shortened. At the moment I'm free so I intend to do it right now."

"Procne's lucky to have you nearby," Philomela said.

"I'm lucky to have her. She's so capable and so much fun. She not only keeps me well grounded, but she also keeps me from taking myself too seriously."

"Yes, she enjoys life and almost always manages to look on the bright side of everything. Mind you, she's having trouble seeing the bright side right now. She knew both murder victims. I suppose you knew them, too."

"I didn't know Annette Murphy, but Kathy Holmes came to see me a couple of times."

"To have clothes altered?" Peripherally, Philomela saw Brent stroll ahead, allowing the two women to talk more freely.

"No. To seek personal advice." Selene looked pensive as if weighing her next words. Then she slowly said, "I suppose it won't hurt to talk to you about it. The second time she came was because of worries about Melvin Springer. They had been dating and she had considered it a light friendship. Apparently, Melvin was starting to put pressure on Kathy to turn their friendship into a commitment. She didn't want that, so she backed off and ended their relationship. It seemed Melvin was devastated and at first threatened to take his own life. She tried to explain that at the moment she was much too career oriented to share her life with someone else. A few days later he saw her out walking with another man and he started phoning her in the middle of the night. She began to fear for his mental state. When she came to me, she actually thought he might do something violent."

"Oh, Selene. What did you do?"

"I wanted her to get a new phone number, but of course she couldn't. Her public number was essential for her work as a realtor. I suggested she talk with the police and ask their advice. At least that way the police would be aware of the problem and might even chat with Melvin about it."

"Did she? Call the police I mean?"

"I don't know. The next day she was murdered."

"Good grief. Do you think Melvin did it?"

"No, as a matter of fact, I don't." Selene shook her head. "I'm sure his suicide threats were a result of having lost Maxine and then being rejected by Kathy."

"Have you told the police about his behavior?"

She shook her head again. "If the police don't come up with a suspect soon, I might do so. But my position is similar to a priest at confession. Kathy expected me to keep her problem confidential."

"A couple of minutes ago you said that now she's gone it's okay to tell me about it."

"Philomela, our religious beliefs may be a bit different, but the basis of them is similar. I believe in a superior power, and I don't know if you do. But I do know you won't blab about Kathy's concerns with anyone else."

"I won't." Gazing steadily at Selene's pale blue eyes, Philomela's abdominal muscles tightened. "Unlike you, I don't get direct messages from the spirit world. I just get the occasional gut feeling. Have you received an out-of-this-world suggestion as to who committed either murder?"

"Nothing yet. That's one reason I hate to put Melvin in the sights of the police. They might focus on him and miss finding who actually did it."

"Yes. False rumors can be ruinous to the person in question." Philomela turned and gazed toward the Salish Sea then suddenly pivoted back to Selene. "You said Melvin saw Kathy out walking with another man."

"Yes."

"Do you know who the man was?"

"Yes, she told me. I won't mention his name because he's married and for the most part, he and his wife are happily married. As far as I know his relationship with Kathy was not romantic. Certainly not a cause for divorce."

"So, the plot thickens."

"Indeed, it does."

"Keep in touch, Selene."

"I will."

Selene walked toward the dress shop and Philomela hurried after Brent. Like a dust devil her thoughts whirled around Melvin Springer and Tom Trust. Trying to make sense of ideas pertaining to the murders, she caught up with her husband.

"So, Philomela, that's your psychic acquaintance. I think you already know half the residents in Saltaire."

"Not half, Brent. But Procne has introduced me to quite a few people."

"In a couple more weeks you'll know everyone."

"Don't be silly. It will take more than a couple of weeks to meet three or four thousand people." She chuckled and stopped beside Brent's truck and opened the passenger door. "Let's go. We have things to do at the grocery store. We might even find a frozen meal that we can cook in the oven tonight."

"What class. Our first dinner in Olympus." He grinned and patted her arm.

CHAPTER 22

Saturday Evening

*H*e looked at the waves lapping against the rocks, pulled the hoodie close to his face and turned around. He surreptitiously raised his small binoculars to his eyes and studied the windows of the five townhouses. He knew each unit had a separate entrance to the outdoors, three of which opened into an open-air vestibule. He knew who lived in all five. Sheila Trust lived with her husband in the top one and their lights were already turned on. In the two units below them, lived Procne Ellis and Selene Hamilton. A dim light shone through Selene's windows, but Procne's were in darkness. He wondered if she was home alone or out with her sister and brother-in-law. He clenched his jaw and glanced without interest at the two lowest level townhouses. A gray-haired couple lived in one and a white-haired widow lived in the other. They lived quietly and didn't warrant his attention.

He still felt confident enough to enjoy interaction with other people. His overpowering passion was at rest and nothing lured him toward satisfying it. To be honest with himself, he sometimes wished it would stay that way.

Right now, he hoped it would remain in this state for months, even for the rest of his life. He had hoped that feeling of peace would happen once before, but the needy desire had slowly risen to the surface and bubbled there until he was forced to allow it to erupt. The imperfect person had to be curtailed. A color-coordinated silk tie efficiently removed the problem. After using the tie once, the action was much easier the second time. Afterward, the anger and passion that had resided within him was relieved and his chance to gain more wealth increased. Once again, he could relax, enjoy social interaction with other people.

That's what he would do now...relax and socially interact with other people. He was good at it. His upbringing had been upper middle-class so he knew how to behave socially. His polite manners, pleasant conversations, and social amenities kept him in demand for dinner parties. On many occasions he was asked to even out the boy-girl ratio around a candle-lit table. But to be honest with himself, he preferred his own company to that of others.

He lowered the binoculars, stuck them in the pocket of his hoodie, and strode along the seashore. He turned onto Main Avenue and at the History Café opened the door and entered.

"Are you still open?" he asked.

Jean, who was busy behind the counter, said, "I am. There was a book reading here this evening. Many people stayed later, drinking hot chocolate and herb tea. I was happy to serve them and receive their payments."

"The readings must be good for business."

"Tonight, the two authors were local mystery writers."

"Ah, I wish I'd known. I'd have come and maybe learned something."

CHAPTER 23

Monday Morning

Philomela, I'm so happy. I still can't believe you and Brent are actually moving to Saltaire."

Her kid sister was so enthusiastic, Philomela couldn't help but smile.

"The sooner you move here the better." Procne spontaneously threw her arms around her sister's shoulders then did the same with Brent. "When will you do it? Move, I mean."

"We finally set a tentative date. In about a month...provided we can book a moving van."

"I'll do that for you." Before Philomela could say yea or nay, Procne jumped in with, "I'll book one online right now."

"What do you think, Brent?" Philomela asked.

"That's fine with me. You'll be doing most of the packing anyway."

"True." Philomela shrugged. "The middle of the month will be best. Less busy than the beginning or end. Most people, especially renters, move on the first day the month."

"Is October fifteenth okay?" Brent and Philomela nodded affirmatively, and Procne sat down at her computer. "Do you have a special moving company in mind?"

"Whatever's handy and available," Philomela replied.

Procne clicked the keyboard and the mouse and rapidly confirmed a date and made arrangements. "There, that's done. Now we can go and eat breakfast." She picked up a many-colored cotton jacket and slipped her arms into its sleeves.

"Procne," Philomela said, "your jacket blends with your olive drab pants and tee-shirt. But its multi-colors brighten your outfit. Very smart."

"See, Brent." Procne nudged her brother-in-law. "Your wife is already becoming fashion conscious. Before you know it, she'll be a magnificent clothes horse."

"I like her the way she is now. I shudder to think what she'll be like after living near you. Our closets will burst at the hinges."

Procne laughed, opened her door to the open-air vestibule and led them to the metal gate. She closed it behind them and they walked toward the sea.

They commented about the raucous songs of seagulls and crows. Near the bronze man who as usual held a fresh flower in his hand, Procne explained to Brent that no one knew who always put the fresh flowers there…except of course the person responsible for doing it.

"It's a mystery," Philomela said.

"I guess it is," Brent said, "Procne, your breakfast invitation ruined Philomela's intention of cooking bacon and eggs in our new kitchen."

"Too bad. But she'll do lots of it after you move here."

Entering the small restaurant, they looked around for an empty table. Procne found one outside on a small deck protruding over the Salish Sea. They sat down and peered into the wavy depths and looked for fish. The waitress interrupted their studies and asked if they would like a beverage. All three ordered coffee and accepted the menus she handed to them. With little ado they all chose Eggs Benedict. The consensus was perfectly rational—it was something they normally didn't eat at home.

Just as the waitress delivered their orders, Tom and Sheila Trust walked through the open door to the deck. Watching them gaze out to the sea, Philomela noticed how Sheila's statuesque figure set off her white and gray dress and white summer jacket. The shop owner could have stepped out of the classiest glamour magazine on the stands. Her fashion sense was impeccable and, like Procne, she had the figure to look good in anything. Of course, Procne's clothes were funkier and more fun that Sheila's, but both women were great advertisers for the shops they each owned. Philomela smiled to herself—after years of noticing only shoes, she was now noticing myriad things about the fashion world.

"Hi, Procne." Sheila smiled and nodded to Philomela and Brent. "Is it warm enough to eat out here?"

"It's fine right now," Procne replied. "The autumn sun still has a lot of warmth but in the shade the ocean breeze might be chilly. Sheila and Tom, you remember my sister and her husband, Brent."

"I certainly do." Being a good realtor Tom promptly asked, "Is your new home still okay?"

"It is," Brent replied. "Procne just booked a moving van for us. We'll be moving here in a month."

"Wonderful." Sheila sat down at the table adjacent to them, put her white clutch purse on her lap, and smiled at

Philomela and Brent. "This is a great town. I'm sure you'll be happy here."

"So far, the only problem is visitors in the basement. Our new neighbor, Mary Skidmore, says a cat will solve our rat problem."

Tom chuckled. "Yes, a cat that's a good hunter will do the job."

"Have you heard anything more about the murder investigations?" Procne gazed first at Sheila then at Tom.

They both shook their heads.

Tom sat on the chair across the table from his wife and focused on Procne. "Members of my staff are on pins and needles. As I told Philomela, they think Trust Realty realtors are the murderer's target. You can imagine how tense our working conditions are. I hope the police soon catch the murderer."

Breakfast proceeded amicably. When Brent and the sisters finished eating their Eggs Benedict and draining the last of their coffee, he paid the bill. Procne argued that she had invited them, but then succumbed when he said she could pay next time. On the way from the deck into the restaurant proper, Brent followed close behind Procne. Philomela lingered for one last look at the undulating water and the flying seabirds then said goodbye to the Trusts and strolled inside the restaurant. Passing a couple sitting at a table for two, she overheard the woman speak.

"They're outside on the deck. The police are keeping a close eye on him. He was seen on several occasions with Kathy Holmes. They always took walks together. No one can verify his whereabouts on the occasion of either murder."

Philomela paused mid-step and heard the man ask, "Were Tom and Kathy an item?"

"Of course they were. But Tom didn't want his wife to know he was having an affair."

"How do you know all this?"

"Daphne told me. Everybody knew. It's common knowledge."

"The question is…why did he kill two of his best employees?"

"Because Kathy dropped him and then because he knew that Annette knew he had killed Kathy."

"Sounds rather nebulous." The man looked up, saw Philomela staring at them and then appearing embarrassed looked away from her.

Philomela wanted to rebut the rampant rumor. But being embarrassed at being caught overtly eavesdropping she held her tongue and continued walking through the restaurant. Outside, she caught up to Procne and Brent and breathlessly told them what she had just heard. "That rumor is getting more outrageous every time I hear it. Being a snoop is starting to raise my ire."

Procne laughed. "The woman is ridiculous. I agree with the man. It's very nebulous. Kathy was friends with lots of people, men included. I doubt there was any hanky-panky going on. Besides, Sheila and Tom have a happy relationship."

Later, Philomela tried to make sense of the gossip she had heard. Rumors could be illogical and often evil. Some were based on imaginative flights of fancy, some developed from envy, others resulted from people puffing up their own importance by putting someone else down, and a few placed guilt on another person to hide their own guilt. She didn't know in what category this last one fit.

She wondered if the implication of Tom Trust had any basis. Who, she wondered, had actually started the rumor? Was it the lady sitting with her husband at the breakfast table? Or had someone else told her, knowing she would repeat it? Did the old adage, "where there's smoke, there's fire," have any bearing? Not necessarily. A smudge had smoke but no fire. And its smoke was beneficial because it repelled mosquitoes.

The two women she had overheard in the History Café had also talked about Kathy Holmes and Tom Trust. They had implied the two had been close friends, not necessarily having an affair. At the street market the couple munching salmon burgers had discussed Melvin Springer as being a suspect, but they had said nothing concrete. Rumors and gossip. That's all there was to any of it.

Then Selene Hamilton came to mind. She was many things, but a gossip was not one of them. She had mentioned the friendship between Tom and Kathy because she intuitively knew Philomela was already aware of the rumor. There was no question in her mind that Selene took Melvin's suicide threat seriously, and Philomela was equally confident he was not the murderer.

In the past Selene had made it clear that she considered her psychic abilities a gift that must not be abused. She seemed to live up to it. People were drawn to her by her honest concern for their problems, be they health, romance, business, finances, or relationships with friends and family. She listened to them, meditated on the problems, and tried to help them. Philomela was confident the psychic did not have a mean bone in her body. But from past experience she knew Selene was a prophet who sometimes hit and sometimes missed.

She also knew Selene didn't expect payment for offering reassurance, comfort, and subtle advice. But she did accept voluntary gifts from people who appreciated her guidance. The gifts included gift certificates, flowers, food, wine, and money. Doubtless the gifts improved her standard of living which relied on past investments as well as her sewing and part time employment in Sheila's and Procne's shops.

As far as the current rumors concerning Melvin and Tom were concerned, Philomela suspected the police also had heard them. She would feel like a fool going to Constable James or Corporal Stinson and telling them fluffs of gossip that probably had no bearing on either case. She decided to zip her lip and keep the rumors to herself. However, that did not mean she would close her eyes and ears to what was happening and being said around her.

She couldn't forget that the two slayings might have been unrelated, committed randomly, and not based on motive. The first killer could have caught a ferry and been long gone from the island, maybe even the country, before the second was committed. Annette's life may have been taken by a copycat killer.

But surely the perpetrator or perpetrators killed for a reason. Five motives came to Philomela's mind. Revenge—alleviating anger at a hurt or supposed hurt. Pride—successfully evading cops in their pursuit of justice. Public acclaim—being discussed by TV personalities, newspaper reporters, the public, and the police. Lack of empathy—unable to identify with the pain his actions caused a person and her loved ones. Power—the thrill of taking the life of an innocent person. A moment later, she added a sixth motive, though she wasn't sure how it could fit what had happened. Greed—the desire for more money and more and more stuff.

She wondered if the perpetrator knew the victim in some capacity. She also considered that drugs and alcohol could make a person behave irrationally, allowing him or her to behave in a manner that would normally be reprehensible. Someone stressed beyond personal capabilities might also spin out of control.

Almost everyone in Saltaire knew, or knew about, the two victims. By now most residents would have heard that the victims had been strangled with a man's tie. But did many people suspect that Melvin and Tom fit the persons of interest group simply because they had had a brief friendship with Kathy? The tie weapon and the strength needed to choke the victim definitely zeroed in on a male perpetrator.

Philomela pondered the idea of sitting down with Procne and Selene and between the three of them writing down the names of all the town's male residents. Doubtless it would be a total waste of time. But then again, they would be doing something and, who knew, in the long run it might aid the investigation.

CHAPTER 24

Tuesday Morning and Afternoon

B efore too long we'll board the ferry, drive to our old home and prepare to move." Brent glanced at the patio furniture then studied his wife. "This doesn't feel like home. At least not yet."

"After this place holds familiar furniture and is stocked with food, we'll consider it home. But, let's face it, Calgary has been our home for a long time."

"And a good home, it was…and at the moment still is."

With a wan smile Philomela nodded agreement. "I'm sure the town of Saltaire and this house will be a good home, too. It will simply depend on our personal outlooks."

"That's the basic truth."

Philomela sipped her coffee then said, "Our coffee-maker came from the hardware store. I rationalized that when the old one from Calgary breaks down, we can use this one."

"Sometimes you're almost frugal."

"Especially when I buy shoes at bargain stores."

They both chuckled. Sitting companionably at the patio table in their dining room, they felt relaxed. No commitments loomed and no tasks needed immediate attention. With their house hunting and house cleaning finished, they felt as if on holiday mode. They were enjoying everything—the patio table and chairs, the coffee and coffee mugs, and the overgrown garden view through the dining room window.

"I promised Procne I'd help at the shop this afternoon. She's busy labeling new fall merchandise. I'll walk over. Have you decided what you'll do?"

"Yup. I'm going to see a man about a car."

"I beg your pardon?" She locked eyes with him.

"I saw an advert for an old Jaguar that's for sale. The owner is a member of the local Jaguar Club. After we move here, I intend to join the club."

"But you already have an old Jaguar."

"How many pairs of shoes do you have?"

"Jags cost more than shoes. And they take up more room."

"Some old Jags aren't terribly expensive. This car is a 1965 vehicle and doesn't cost much. I suspect restorative work has to be done on it. Don't worry. I won't buy it. At least not right now."

"Cars. A hobby for retirement. No wonder you want a three car garage."

His head bobbed affirmatively. "I'm thinking of the future. In the meantime, there's no harm in looking."

"None whatsoever."

That afternoon, at Whimsical Woman, Philomela worked as saleslady so Procne could hole up in the back office pricing new garments and preparing another fall order. Every so often she came out front to ask any customer who was interested, if they had a preference for a specific winter garment. She wanted to please the local shoppers.

Finally, Procne strolled over to her sister who was arranging jackets in order of size. "I'm finished. What's new?"

'Nothing much. I sold a blouse, a cardigan sweater, and a pair of pants with flared legs."

"Awesome. What's new with you?"

Yesterday I bought a coffeemaker at the hardware store. Our patio furniture in the dining room is working well."

"You've been busy. Patio furniture in the dining room is very clever."

"I think so. Actually, I can hardly wait to move it outside on the back patio. What about you? Anything new and exciting in your life?"

"Not really. Oh yeah, I forgot to tell you about Sunday night. It was twilight, getting dark, and I looked out the window. A man with binoculars stood on the sea-walk studying our townhouse building. I wondered if he was casing the joint to break in and perform a robbery. Or maybe to murder someone. It was creepy."

"Did he focus on your townhouse?"

"He seemed as interested in Selene's as in mine.

"Did you recognize him?"

"No. He was wearing a hoodie. I couldn't see his face or his head."

"What about size? Was he tall? Short? Of medium girth? Fat? Slim?"

"There wasn't anything to compare him with. But I'd say he was of slim build and of medium height."

"I agree with you. Creepy." Philomela felt her abdominal muscles contract. She studied her sister for a moment. "Did he see you watching him?"

"I don't think so. I hadn't turned on any lights yet. With my dark hair, black cotton sweater, and black tights, I probably blended in with the dark room."

"That's good." Philomela smiled, trying to hide a growing feeling of concern. With the murders of two single women in mind, she didn't like to hear of someone studying the homes of two other single women, especially not her sister's. Though capable people, Selene and Procne would have trouble fighting off a strong, muscular man, especially if he had a man's necktie.

"You look worried," Procne said. "Do you think he could be a problem?"

"Not likely." Philomela faked a smile. "But because of Kathy and Annette, you'd be wise to keep your doors locked and your phone handy. If someone should break in you must scream at the top of your lungs, press 911, and even hit the alarm on your car remote. That would make enough noise to attract attention and scare off an intruder."

Procne laughed. "I hadn't thought of a car remote as part of a residence security system. But it might help."

"Is there anything special you want me to do right now?"

"Not really. But I'm dying for a cup of coffee. Would you mind keeping the shop while I dash to the History Café?"

"No problem."

"Do you want one?"

"Okay. I've only had one today so I shouldn't get caffeine twitches."

Procne hurried out the door and disappeared. A customer came inside and Philomela greeted her and asked if she could be of any help. The customer confessed to just browsing, so Philomela nodded and left her to her own devices. The browsing paid off—the customer left the shop carrying a rusty-orange bag with a summer jacket inside.

Once again, the shop was empty of customers. Philomela sat down on the chair near the cash counter and counted her blessings. Right now, she had more than a few—a husband and sister she loved, a new home, and the prospects of living in a delightful town.

The bell tingled and Philomela looked over at the newcomer. It was Constable James. Philomela stood up, greeted her warmly and mentioned the lovely weather. Then she asked, "Are you having any success with the two murder investigations?"

"Not as much as I'd like."

Deciding this was as good a time as any to broach the rumors, Philomela looked into the constable's gray-blue eyes. "I assume you've heard the rumors roaring around town."

The constable shook her head. "No, I haven't."

"I don't hold any credence in them, but you probably should know about them. According to one rumor, Tom Trust and Kathy Holmes had some sort of relationship. The other rumor claims that Kathy and Melvin Springer comprised an item and then Kathy dumped him."

"Actually, I was aware of the first rumor and have already checked it out. Tom said the rumor is based on him giving Kathy fatherly advice over a personal problem. The second rumor probably has no bearing on the case, but I'll check it out too, just to be sure."

"My sister Procne told me of seeing a man in a hoodie using binoculars to check the townhouse building where she lives. As you may recall, Selene Hamilton and Procne each have a townhouse on the main floor of the building. Two single women each living alone. Procne doesn't think the man saw her because she had not yet turned on a light. The room was darker than the outside twilight."

"I suppose she couldn't recognize him because of the hoodie."

"Correct."

"I'll suggest that a cruiser drive by with special attention to the building. We don't want any more murders."

At that moment, Procne breezed into the shop. "Hello, Constable James. If I had known you were here, I'd have bought three cups of coffee."

"Thanks anyway. But I'm coffee'd out for today. Your sister just told me about an unknown man studying your townhouse building."

Procne looked with surprise at Philomela. "Did you think it important enough to bother the constable with it?"

"Definitely. She should be aware of what's happening in town. She's looking after the welfare of all of us."

"Goodness, you make me sound important." A flush rose from Constable James's neck to her forehead.

"You are important," Philomela said. "We're counting on you to apprehend the murderer and thereby protect all of us."

"We're certainly worried about it," she confessed. "Motives are lacking or are confusing. Sexual? Rejection? Jealousy? Revenge? We hardly know what to think."

"Sexual?" Philomela's eyes widened in surprise. "Were the two victims sexually violated?"

"Oh, oh." Constable James put her hand over her mouth. "I shouldn't have mentioned it. Please don't tell anyone else. We think the choking came first followed by sexual penetration. The crime scene nauseated me. Even Corporal Stinson was affected, and he's witnessed more bad scenes than I have."

"So, at least you know for sure the perpetrator is male. That narrows the field of suspects by half."

Constable James nodded. "I shouldn't be discussing this with you. We want to keep these details from becoming public. There are always a few braggarts who want notoriety so they will confess to a murder they didn't commit. It's easy to eliminate them because, even though they watch TV and read the papers, they don't know exactly what happened."

"Mums the word." Philomela looked over at her sister.

"Right." Procne placed her thumb and index finger along her lips. "Constable James, did you come here to discuss the murders with us?"

"As a matter of fact, I came to take advantage of your sale and buy a casual summer dress. When I'm off duty, I sometimes like to toss off my uniform and dress like a lady."

"Understandable. The forty percent off items are at the back of the store." Procne led her to a rack of colorful summer clothes. "A few are suitable for all seasons. Browse to your heart's content. If you want help, Philomela and I are at your beck and call."

The constable looked from Procne to Philomela and smiled. "If you hear any other rumors, see any more strange happenings, or develop any new theories about the murders, please contact me. I appreciate all types of information. You never know what might turn out to be helpful." She turned to the rack and flicked through the clothes. "Oh, this is my size. How nice to look at dresses instead of at crime scenes."

CHAPTER 25

Procne locked the shop, strolled beside Philomela along Main Avenue, and glanced at cars cruising by. She waved at other shop owners locking up for the night and gazed at restaurateurs preparing for the onslaught of evening diners.

"Hello, sisters."

Startled, Procne turned around and stared at Roger Thistle. "Oh, hi, Roger. Long time no see. How are you doing?" She noted a black band circling his upper arm but refrained from mentioning it.

"With other staff members at Trust Realty, I'm in mourning. It's not a happy time."

"It's a terrible time for everyone in Saltaire." Procne shook her head, still disinclined to believe what had happened to the two young women. "Kathy and Annette didn't deserve to be killed."

"I guess you're right." Roger looked from Procne to Philomela. "Is everything okay at your new house?"

"Yes, thanks. Everything's fine. I think we'll be quite happy there."

"At least one good thing has happened." He turned back to Procne and gave her a half smile. "It's good luck that I ran into you. Actually, I was hoping to catch you before you left your shop. Melvin Springer just phoned me and suggested a few of us have dinner at the hotel dining room. It would be sort of a wake for the two women. I was hoping you would be free…and would come as my date. Are you interested?"

"Tonight?"

"Yeah. I know it's short notice, but it's a spur of the moment thing. I could pick you up at six-thirty. We can either walk over to the hotel or go in my car. Your choice."

"Well…"

"I think Melvin's devastated about Kathy's death. He needs to chat with other people who knew and liked her. And then of course there's Annette."

"She was well liked, too." Procne looked at him pensively. "The rumor is going around that Kathy and Melvin were dating and she broke it off. Some people are even wondering if that triggered Melvin to do the dirty."

"I hadn't heard that. I knew he'd taken her out a couple of times, but I have no idea if they were serious or not. Both gave the impression they were just friends." He glanced at his watch. "Ten after five. What do you say about this evening?"

She shrugged. "Why not? I have nothing on and the food at the hotel is usually good."

"And of course the company will be charming." He smiled broadly.

"Of course. That goes without saying. Roger, you're always charming. And Melvin is always polite."

He bent forward in a mock bow. "I'll buzz you at six-thirty."

Before Procne could reply, Philomela said, "This is where I part company with you folks to walk to my new abode. "Nice to see you, Roger. Bye Sis."

"Thanks again for helping out."

"You're welcome. Take care, Procne." Philomela's green eyes gazed into her sister's sky-blue ones. "And I'm serious."

CHAPTER 26

Tuesday Evening

True to his word, Roger buzzed Procne's intercom at six-thirty.

Carrying a blue cardigan that blended with her blue and white short-sleeved dress, she opened the door, locked it, and hurried to the metal gate. "Is it still my choice to walk or drive?"

"Certainly," Roger replied.

"Let's walk." She slung her cardigan over her shoulder. "I don't need this sweater right now, but I might need it later when walking home." She opened the metal gate and came closer to Roger. Moving together toward the sea-walk, she glanced at the eastern sky above the ocean. "Oh, look. The moon is rising. Another month and it will be a big harvest moon."

"A beautiful sight and a beautiful lady. Just what every man needs."

"You're becoming quite poetic" She glanced at the black band on his upper arm. "Does everyone at Trust Realty wear a black armband?"

"Yes. A dark cloud surrounds all of us."

"Losing one realtor is bad enough. Losing two is…tragic. Are you able to get any work done?"

"I have a couple of new clients who don't know about the murders yet. I try to be cheerful."

"Not easy, I'm sure." She thought of Melvin Springer, the organizer of this unofficial wake, and wondered if he had developed romantic intentions regarding Annette. Probably not. Perhaps he thought sharing stories about Kathy and Annette would help everyone cope with the loss of the two young women. She glanced sideways at Roger. "Do you know who else will be at the dinner tonight?"

"I don't know for sure. Melvin Springer, of course, maybe Tom and Sheila Trust, Jean Greenfield if she can get away from her café, and another realtor from our office. He's new and I can't remember his name."

"What about Selene Hamilton?"

"Did Selene know the victims?"

"She knew Kathy. I'm not sure about Annette. Kathy came to visit her at least once."

"Oh? Why?"

"I got the impression it was a personal matter. Selene doesn't say much about her visitors. She's the inverse of a gossip monger."

"Is she any good as a psychic?"

"Sometimes she's amazing. Often, she casually makes statements that later prove to be true. Sometimes she's a bit airy-fairy, but most people say her advice hits the mark. She spends a lot of time listening."

"Mmm. Have you ever consulted her?"

"Not really. But we're neighbors and she often says things to me that later prove to be pertinent. More than once she gave me glimpses into the future that helped me make decisions."

"I don't hold much faith in all that psychic stuff."

"A lot of people think it's all balderdash."

"But you don't?"

"I have an open mind about it. I've seen enough to make me think something more than luck or coincidence is involved."

"Well, to each his own."

Arriving at the hotel dining room, they looked around and saw three other mourners—Melvin, Sheila and Tom. As Roger and Procne approached their table, Melvin and Tom politely stood up. Greetings were in process when a man and woman arrived. Tom introduced them. Procne caught their first names—Jim and Sue—Jim had joined Trust Realty four weeks ago and Sue was his wife. A few minutes later Myrtle, the oldest realtor at Trust Realty, arrived. Sheila fussed over her and shifted Myrtle's cutlery into a new order—Procne wasn't sure to what purpose. Drinks flowed and conversation hummed pleasantly. They discussed the good weather, the street market, and the lessening of summer tourists. Melvin mentioned that his favorite warm weather drink, gin and tonic, would soon be replaced with his favorite winter drink, Scotch whisky and a dash of water.

"Someone who loved her gin was the English queen mom, now deceased." Procne put her hand over her mouth and mumbled, "Oops."

"Now deceased." Melvin smiled wanly at Procne. "That's why we're here. To remember the vibrant lives of Kathy Holmes and Annette Murphy."

From there, conversation about the two young women flowed easily. Everyone had known and liked Kathy, even the newcomers. Amusing and flattering anecdotes were told about her job activities, her good business sense, her care and involvement with clients, her sense of humor, her fashionable clothes, and her professional appearance and behavior. They also knew Annette, but not as well as they knew Kathy. They agreed she had been a joy to be with and her work ethic was such that she probably would have become a first class-realtor.

"Though young, she was up and coming," Tom said. "She had all the right qualities—diligence, lovely personality, and the enthusiasm and energy of youth."

After finishing her main course, Procne excused herself and made her way toward the necessary room. Halfway down the hall she heard a male voice call "Procne." Whirling one hundred and eighty degrees she saw Melvin hurrying to catch up with her. She waited for him.

"What do you think?" he asked. "Are we doing the right thing?"

"Yes, Melvin. I think your idea was brilliant. Having a…a wake is just what's needed to help us accept the sad situation. You must have sensed that people who knew the victims wanted to talk and remember nice things about them."

"I know I felt that way." He smiled at her and his smile reached his eyes. "Procne, I had briefly dated both of them. I was attracted to Kathy, but there was no spark between Annette and me. However, they both were pleasant companions."

She nodded.

"Eating alone all the time is fine, but sometimes a bit of company is a nice diversion. I had hoped an intimate relationship between Kathy and me would develop. It didn't, but I still hoped it might. Now, of course, that hope is gone forever."

She nodded again and started to walk toward her destination.

He kept up with her and said, "I'm glad you understand. I knew you would." She turned to go her separate way. "Procne, would you go with me to Saltaire Island for a picnic on Sunday?"

Surprised, she turned and wide-eyed stared at him. "A picnic? On Sunday? On Saltaire Island?"

"Yes. The weather forecast is good."

"I haven't been to that island since my first year here." She glanced down at his shiny brown shoes and neatly pressed pants then looked up at his dark eyes. He didn't strike her as a picnic sort of guy. "Well, I'm free on Sunday. So why not? If the weather is nice a picnic could be fun."

"I'll talk with Jean Greenfield and buy the food at the History Café. You won't have to worry about anything."

"Jean's food is bound to be delicious. I'll bring water and a thermos of coffee."

"Great. I'll pick you up at ten-thirty and we'll catch the eleven o'clock ferry."

"Okay." She glanced at the female stick figure on the washroom door and said, "I'll see you back in the dining room." Entering the necessary room, she thought about Saltaire Island.

The small island was barely a kilometer from the town and enjoyed the same name. It could have been an extension of the town except its only accesses were by boat and helicopter. The sandy beach was wide and long, and she recalled the tidal pools as being fascinating. Some were deep enough for a child to swim in. The path through a primeval forest was exotic and several homes with private jetties existed on the far side of the island. Day trippers seldom went near them.

She returned to the dining area and about ten minutes later the new realtor and his wife departed. The others were eating dessert and sipping decaf coffee when Jean Greenfield and a young lady arrived. Jean greeted everyone breathlessly, introduced her friend Cindy, and then sat down at the table with a sigh of obvious relief.

"Oh, my aching feet," she said. "We had such a busy evening. I wasn't sure I'd get here."

"We're glad you made it." Procne's lips turned slightly up at the corners. "Being busy is a good thing."

"Yes, it is," Jean said. "The customers were interesting and the money isn't to be sneezed at. Cindy and I no longer go out alone, especially in the evening, so we're sticking together like a sealed envelope." Jean looked up at a waitress. "I'd like to have dessert, please. Crème Brule." As Cindy ordered, Jean gazed questioningly at everyone seated at the table. Then she asked, "Has anyone solved the two murders yet?"

"I'm afraid not." Melvin shook his head despondently. "I don't think the police even have a prime suspect."

"Too bad. Every woman who comes into the History Café is nervous about a murderer being on the loose. We'll all breathe easier after he's caught." Jean gazed at Sheila, Myrtle, and Procne.

"Male realtors will breathe easier, too," Tom said. "Especially realtors at my firm."

"Everyone will be relieved." Melvin gazed at the waitress setting deserts in front of the two newcomers. When she left he said, "Who knows what the murderer is thinking? Maybe he or she just loves killing and doesn't care who the victim is."

"Everyone in the entire area is on edge." Sheila's palms pressed against both her cheeks. "Saltaire is too nice a place to be wrapped in fear. Why did the murderer have to do his evil deeds here instead of elsewhere?"

"That's the sixty-four-thousand-dollar question," Procne said.

"Who dunnit?" Jean asked. "And why had he dunnit? Assuming of course the killer is a "he." She raised her spoon and took a bite of Crème Brule.

No one came up with an answer. Nor did anyone seem eager to leave the table. Procne could feel the warm camaraderie growing warmer. It felt protective, making her feel safe in the present company. She could have stayed longer, but the thought of getting to work on time tomorrow morning took precedence. Finally, she stood up and thanked Melvin on behalf of everyone there for organizing the mini-wake.

"I enjoyed a delicious dinner and the companionship has made me feel a little better. Though the victims will never be brought back to life, talking about the tragic loss with friends will help to bring something resembling closure. Kathy and Annette may be gone but they aren't forgotten. Personally, after this evening, I feel better equipped to carry on with my ordinary, day by day life." Procne sat down.

The assembly put their hands together and clapped. They each paid their respective dinner bills then exchanged physical hugs and verbal good nights.

Roger eased over to Procne. "I'll walk you home."

"You don't have to do that." Tom's quick intervention surprised Procne. "Sheila and I have the same destination as Procne. She can walk home with us."

"There's an old saying—*A nice girl leaves a party with the fellow who brung her.*" Roger chuckled. "And I brung her."

"I think you made up that saying," Sheila said.

"No," Roger said. "I first heard it as a teen-ager. But I don't remember where or when or who said it."

"It sounds like an old song." Sheila laughed. "Roger, you're waxing poetic tonight."

"That's what Procne said earlier." He looked up at the sky. "Twinkling stars and a half moon. No wonder I want to walk a pretty girl home."

"We'll enjoy walking with Procne, too." Sheila stepped up to Procne and adjusted her sweater. "That's better."

"Always the fashionista," Procne said, accepting the sweater adjustment.

Tom moved to Procne's side. "We all need lots of sleep in order to cope with the brunt of the two tragedies."

"I won't argue about needing sleep," Roger said. "However, I insist on taking Procne home." He stepped between Tom and Procne.

Feeling like a desirable princess being wooed by two princes, Procne grinned. "All four of us can walk together. I agree with Roger. The stars and moon are beautiful. They even reflect on the calm water of the Salish Sea."

Roger took hold of her arm and they moved forward together. Sheila and Tom fell into step behind them and all four walked from the hotel restaurant to the townhouse complex. At the metal gate Tom stopped, unlocked it, and pulled it open. He held it open as the other three walked into the open-air vestibule. Sheila bade the two single people goodnight and disappeared into their unit. Tom lingered and watched Procne unlock her door.

"Is it too late to invite me in for a nightcap?" Roger asked her.

"Like Tom said—we need our sleep—and I have a busy day tomorrow. Besides, I don't drink alcohol at bedtime."

"Maybe we could have dinner and go to a movie some time."

"That would be nice. Wake or not, I enjoyed this evening, Roger. Thanks for asking me to join the group." She stepped into the open doorway and waved her fingers at him. "Thanks, too, for walking me home." She started to close the door.

"You're welcome." He edged closer to the open space and seemed to peer inside.

"Goodnight you two," Tom said, still standing beside his own door.

"Goodnight, Tom." It crossed her mind that he was behaving in a strange manner, almost possessively.

For no good reason she hurriedly closed the door and locked it.

It wasn't because of Roger or Tom that she had hurriedly locked the door. It was because her thoughts suddenly pictured the unknown man peering through binoculars at her townhouse. Who was he? He had been unnerving then and the thought of him was unnerving now. Surely he wasn't Tom or Roger. She hoped the hoodie man wouldn't make her feel ill at ease with every man she knew. That would be a dreadful way to live.

Then she thought of her son, her brother-in-law, and the museum curator. She didn't feel ill at ease with them. That brought her thinking back in perspective.

CHAPTER 27

Wednesday Morning

Philomela and Brent ate a light breakfast and debated whether to be tourists in their new hometown or homeowners in their neglected garden. Leaving their plans in limbo, Philomela finished eating her first meal of the day, tidied up the kitchen, and strolled out the back door. Standing on the patio, she looked up at the pristine blue sky then down at the forest of unknown shrubs and weeds.

"The garden needs us," she said.

Outside, the aromatic soft air filled her lungs and the sun warmed her face and legs. She was glad she had put on a pair of shorts. She strolled across the lawn to a grass and weed filled flowerbed. Bending down she studied the plants then pulled a few undesirable ones.

Brent's voice startled her. "Did I ever mention that you have nice legs?"

She crooked her head and saw him standing by the back door. "Do you realize I've had the same pair of legs for over fifty years?" Seeing his lips form an upward crescent, she added, "The geriatric experts say the legs are the last to go."

"What's the first?"

"Let's not worry about that."

Brent grinned, left the patio and joined her. He picked up bits of paper that winds had blown against trees and shrubs and put them in the garbage bin. He puttered around two trees and asked if they were a hazelnut tree and an apple.

"One is an apple. I don't know about the other one." She busily secured grape vines growing along a wire trellis and cleaned up droppings from the fig tree located on the south side of the garage. "The next thing I'm going to do is buy is a west coast gardening book."

"The next thing I'm going to do is buy is a bunch of tools. There isn't much we can accomplish until we have spades, hoes, secateurs, rakes, and a lawnmower. But I hate to go out and purchase too much when our existing ones will soon be here. We don't need duplicates."

"I agree. We already have too much stuff." She looked around at the overgrown garden and shrugged. "There's not much else we can do right now. Why don't we be tourists and visit the Marine Center?"

"What's that? And where is it?"

"It's a museum of sea life and it's a block off Main Avenue. A five minute walk from here."

At the Marine Center, Brent bought tickets from a lady sitting behind a counter and he and Philomela entered a huge elevator. A minute later a voice announced they would be descending. The door closed and suddenly everything started to jump, rattle and shake. Sounds of running water filled their ears and Philomela looked up and watched water swirl outside the glass roof. The rattling and shaking finally stopped and the back door opened exposing a spacious hallway.

Philomela and Brent walked into the hall, looked at a few people and listened to soft voices. Walking forward they stared at displays built into the walls.

"What beautiful dioramas," Philomela said. "And look at the different sea creatures and the variety of plants." Reading a sign explaining their unique features, she was distracted by the voice of a woman walking over to the adjacent display.

"I hope the police soon find the killer."

The words prompted Philomela to look over at a man and woman who seemed more intent on their conversation than on the sea-life in front of their eyes.

"I'm sure the police are doing everything they can." The man stared blankly at his companion.

Philomela leaned toward them, surreptitiously listening to their words.

"Annette's mother is beside herself," the woman said. "When I visited her yesterday, she was a basket case. She kept saying, 'This isn't the way things should happen. I'm supposed to go before my daughter.' She worried that Annette might have suffered before dying, and that made her burst into tears. Nothing I could say or do was of any help." The woman shook her head back and forth. "I also wonder if Annette's death was quick. The police haven't given the media or the family any details."

"The media know where she died, and that's about it," the man said.

"And the family knows no more."

Peripherally, Philomela saw the woman take a tissue from her purse, dab her eyes, and blow her nose. Then she and her companion silently moved on to another aquatic display.

Distracted from the dioramas by their conversation, Philomela's thoughts unwontedly focused on the murder. She, too, wondered if the victims had suffered for a period of time. She hoped not. A slow movement caught her eye and the sad thoughts faded from her mind. An octopus, whose colors blended with rocks and gravel and plants, slowly extended one of its eight tentacles.

"Brent," she grabbed his arm. "Look at the octopus. It's amazing. I wouldn't have seen him if he hadn't moved. What incredible camouflage. Could we possibly have evolved from such an interesting creature?"

Brent's head moved negatively. "Evolutionists think we evolved from sea life. Somewhere along the way we must have lost four appendages. Darwin tried to make it all seem logical, but I'm not positive he succeeded."

"I know what you mean. Each creature's anatomy and physiology are so complicated. I often suspect a superior intelligence designed all of us."

Brent chuckled. "I'm not going to debate that issue. Not now at any rate."

Their tour ended at a feeling-trough designed for children. They watched three youngsters put their hands in the water, touch bits of sea life, and loudly exclaim "Ewe" and "Ah."

A few minutes later, in the inevitable gift shop, Philomela examined several crafty items. Buying a small change purse in the shape of an Orca, she asked the salesclerk, "Do you know why Orcas are called Killer Whales?"

"Probably because they eat seals," the clerk replied.

Brent checked his watch and asked, "What now? It's after twelve. Do we have anything to eat at home?"

"Slim pickings. Fruit, lettuce, tomatoes, cold ham." Before he had a chance to reply, she added, "Let's go to the History Café."

"To snoop or to eat?"

"To eat, of course." As an afterthought she confessed, "And to glean tiny bits of information." Brent rolled his eyes and Philomela grinned. "As you already know,

Jean's a fountain of information and she avoids gross gossip and silly speculation."

"Yeah, she supposedly deals with facts. How do you know they really are facts?"

"Because Jean says they are."

He rolled his eyes again.

One fact remained—Philomela was curious and wanted to learn about new developments. So far, Jean was her best source of information. Philomela didn't expect to solve the murders, but because her powers of observation and intuition had assisted police in the past, she hoped they might do so again. She knew from experience that inconsequential bits of information often gelled in her mind and formed unexpected theories—theories that proved constructive. Perhaps her brain was wired differently from most people, causing her to think differently—more or less out-of-the-box.

CHAPTER 28

Wednesday Noon

H
ello, you two. Good to see you." From behind the counter, Jean Greenfield cheerfully welcomed Brent and Philomela and showed interest in their activities. "Are you settled in your new home?"

Philomela shook her head. "Not yet, Jean. And we won't be settled for another month, not until our furniture arrives from Calgary. Right now, we're camping inside a rather empty building."

"That's a good way to camp. Better than camping outside in the cold. When do you expect to make the big move?"

"We plan to go back to Calgary in a couple of weeks. We'll have a garage sale and give accumulated stuff to a thrift shop. Then we'll pack up what's left."

"I don't envy you. The thought of moving unnerves me. I've lived in the same house for almost twenty-four years. I have a lot of stuff that should be thrown out. But I can't seem to do it. To be honest, I hope to go out of my house feet first."

"Seventy years from now," Philomela said.

Jean's eyes twinkled. "That would make me...let's

see…a hundred and fourteen years old."

Philomela grinned. Gazing into the café owner's twin-kling eyes, she grew serious. "Any news about the murders?"

"Nothing…at least nothing new. Constable James confirmed that a man's tie was the weapon in both cases. Last night at the hotel dining room I met with a few people…including your sister…for a memorial to both victims. They ate dinner, but because we were busy here Cindy and I got there just in time for dessert. The event was a modern-day version of an old-fashioned wake. Each of us eulogized Kathy and Annette, and we drank toasts and wished them bon voyage to wherever their souls were going."

"Yesterday after work Procne and I were leaving Whimsical Woman when Roger Thistle suggested she join them. He said Melvin Springer had instigated the dinner."

"Yes, he had. You two should have come." Jean smiled at Brent.

"We weren't invited," he said.

"Our acquaintance with both women was very brief," Philomela said. "But they were the last people on earth I would have expected to be murdered. Was anyone at the wake able to finger a prime suspect?"

Jean shook her head. "No, though we speculated about it. We unanimously concluded the killer must be some-one from away. Personally, I think it was a man." She shrugged and leaned close to Philomela. "But then again, I don't have any facts to prove it."

"I suppose an element of surprise could have given a strong woman enough advantage to do the dastardly deed," Philomela said.

"That's possible." Jean nodded, looked up at the ceiling then stared directly at Philomela. "Do you have any clues?"

"Not one. If I knew more about the actual crime scenes I might come up with a suspect. So far, I only know both women worked for Trust Realty and both were strangled in houses advertised on multi-listings. We no longer have to speculate about the murder weapon. We know the weapon in both cases was a man's tie. The police are keeping other information close to their chest."

"Well, I'll keep my ear to the ground." Jean threw back her shoulders and in a businesslike manner asked, "What can I get you folks to eat and drink?"

Philomela and Brent ordered bacon, lettuce and tomato sandwiches. They moved over to one of two empty tables and sat down just as four people grabbed the other empty one.

Eating their BLTs, Philomela and Brent chatted about the sea life they had just seen. Occasionally Philomela glanced around, hoping to be enlightened by remarks from nearby diners. Nothing of interest reached her eardrums.

CHAPTER 29

Wednesday Afternoon

After lunch, as Philomela strolled side by side with Brent along Main Avenue, she noticed a sign, 'Cut and Curl.' Looking through the window, her eyes focused on a clean, neat hair salon. At the moment it contained no client in any of three work areas.

"My red mop needs to be trimmed," she said to Brent. "Hang on for a minute while I dash in and make an appointment."

Inside the salon, she hurried over to a young lady who was sweeping up clumps of hair from the floor and asked, "Could I make an appointment for a wash and trim?"

Startled, the girl almost dropped her broom. "I didn't hear you enter the salon. When do you want to come?"

Philomela glanced around. "Right now?"

"That would be okay. My next appointment phoned an hour ago to cancel because of a bad cold."

"How serendipitous for me. I'll run out and tell my husband not to wait. Be back in a jiffy." Outside she said, "Good news, Brent. She'll take me right now."

"Maybe I'll look for a barber. I need a cut, too."

"Definitely. Your hair is so long it almost touches your ears. Another two years and it might hit your shoulders."

He ignored her sarcasm. "We both have keys to Olympus. I'll see you there in an hour or so."

With a four-finger wave she turned and re-entered Cut and Curl.

The young girl guided her to one of two hair-washing sinks. "My name is Sherry," she said and proceeded to spray Philomela's hair with water. Her fingers massaged shampoo onto her client's scalp and she chatted merrily about the sunny weather. Then she asked if Philomela lived in Saltaire or was visiting.

"As a matter of fact, a few days ago my husband and I bought a house. We were looked after by Trust Realty."

"Oh." Sherry's eyes widened. "Did you meet Kathy or Annette?"

"Actually, we initially dealt with Kathy. After her death Roger Thistle took over. But Annette was the one who found a house that suited us. And then she completed the deal."

Sherry turned off the taps, wrapped a towel around Philomela's head, and guided her to a swivel chair in front of a large mirror. "Annette and I went to high school together. What happened to her is unbelievable. She's the first person in our class to die. I can't believe she was murdered." Sherry's entire body shuddered, and a small moan erupted between her lips.

Feeling empathy for the young girl, Philomela had an urge to spread her arms and give the girl a hug. But she stopped herself for fear of being unduly intimate. Instead she nodded her head and sat down on the swivel chair.

Sherry cleared her throat and in a businesslike manner unwound the towel from Philomela's head and started to comb her hair. "Three high school friends came over to my place last night and we drank two bottles of wine. We were awfully upset. I still am. Annette was the nicest person you could ever meet. She was smart yet kind and considerate. Everyone loved her. Why would anyone want to kill her?"

"No one seems able to answer that question," Philomela replied. "I hope the police will soon be able to do so."

"Last night we wondered if one of us would be next on the killer's list. The four of us, as well as Annette, graduated in the same class. Kathy was fifteen years ahead of us." She brushed Philomela's hair vigorously, almost in anger. "So far, the killer has attacked only females who graduated from our high school."

"Good grief. A lot of realtors feel the same way you do. So far, the killer has targeted only realtors who work at Trust Realty."

"Oh, I hadn't thought of that." Sherry bit her lower lip then picked up her scissors and started trimming the ends of Philomela's hair. "Is your hair naturally this shade of red?"

"Just about. For the last couple of years, a dye bottle of vibrant red has enhanced the color and covered numerous strands of white."

"The color looks pretty with your skin shade."

"Thanks. My skin's not very pretty when it sunburns. Then I look like a boiled lobster. But of course the sun, in moderation, provides Vitamin D."

"The good and the bad." Sherry chuckled and continued snipping. She finally set the scissors on her table and began to blow dry Philomela's hair. She swiveled the chair around and handed her client a hand mirror.

Seeing the back of her head in the mirror, Philomela said, "That's much better."

As she returned the hand mirror to Sherry, a young girl entered the shop and breathlessly said, "Oh, Sherry, sorry to be late. The police kept asking me all sorts of questions about Annette."

"It's okay, Collette, your client hasn't arrived yet. What did the police want?"

"They didn't actually say. But they seemed to imply that Annette had been raped. Besides being choked to death, that is."

"Omigod, Collette." Obviously shocked, Sherry almost dropped the hand mirror.

Philomela was also shocked. "Did the police actually say she had been raped?" she asked.

"Not really. They asked me all kinds of questions about whether she had a steady boyfriend and whether she was free and easy with her sexual favors. Why would they be interested in such things if she was just choked to death?"

Philomela shrugged and studied the newcomer's face. The young girl's expansive white cornea accented her dark pupils, making her look both surprised and wide awake. "Your idea of rape puts a different light on the murder, doesn't it?"

"It makes it worse for Annette," Sherry said. "And scarier for us girls."

"Was Annette promiscuous?" Philomela asked.

"Not at all," Sherry replied. "In fact, you could say she was a bit tight-assed about such things."

Philomela's tongue was silent but her thoughts raced. Apparently, the killer was not trying to remove the world of prostitutes and loose women. Now the question uppermost in her mind was—why would someone kill an upstanding, innocent young woman? And was rape an issue?

She mentally answered her own question. Perhaps the killer's desire was to enjoy having the power over someone's life and death. To put it blunter, the killer wanted to watch a person die at his hands. Or perhaps a male sought revenge on all females because he hated his mother. Or the murderer could have been mentally disturbed or else so zonked out with drugs he didn't understand what he was doing. Or was the perpetrator a female who envied another woman's popularity or beauty?

No, not a woman, not if rape was involved.

"What else did the police ask you?" Philomela's intuition was working overtime.

Still wide-eyed, Collette stared at Philomela. "Corporal Stinson wondered if Annette was part of the drug scene. I assured him she wasn't. We once saw one of our classmates go cuckoo after taking crystal meth—he tried to fly out a window. He fell one story and luckily only broke a leg and an arm. After seeing his stupid antics all of us avoided street drugs like the plague."

"A wise decision," Philomela said. "Did the police ask you any other questions?"

"Constable James gave me her business card and asked me to phone if I thought of anything else, no matter how silly it might seem. She said small things often prove helpful in pinpointing the culprit."

"I'm sure that's true." Philomela nodded her head in confirmation. "So, both of you girls were good friends with Annette."

"The best," Sherry said.

"I liked her, too. She was a good realtor, pleasant, ingenious, and capable. I'm indebted to her for finding the perfect house for us. I'm sure Trust Realty will miss her."

"I wonder who will be the next victim." Sherry shuddered.

CHAPTER 30

Wednesday Evening.

Procne poured a small glass of Retsina. She took a sip and savored the Greek wine's Aleppo pine flavor. Being one of the rare people who truly enjoyed the wine's pine-resin taste, she felt special, probably because her Greek grandfather had introduced it to her. She recalled how he had diluted a six-ounce glass of water with three ounces of wine for Philomela on her eighteenth birthday. The glass he had handed to Procne, his younger granddaughter, had been water with a few drops of Retsina.

"Sip it slowly and let your mouth enjoy the flavor," he had said. Then he had added, "Never drink too much."

Procne had felt very grown up, but her reaction had been juvenile. After swallowing a small mouthful, she had said, "Yuk" and screwed up her nose.

Times changed. Now she liked the wine—undiluted with water. And whenever she drank it, she thought of her wise grandfather.

In the sitting room, she set her glass on the coffee table and sat down on the nearest sofa. It was nice to relax. The day had been busy. Her end-of-summer sale was a huge success, enhancing her bank account and giving her shop more space for fall and winter garments. The weather, still warm and sunny, had prompted customers to take advantage of the good prices. Doubtless they intended to wear the outfits now as well as save some for next spring. Locals, having received her thirty-percent-off email, had responded by entering the shop in droves. Tourists, seeing the sale sign in the window, wandered inside to browse and usually ended up exchanging money for garments.

The summer stock was thinning and some of her winter orders had already arrived. Next week she planned to put the remaining summer clothes on a forty-percent-off rack. The rest of the shop would be devoted to displays of cool and cold weather clothing. The changing season was good for the owner of a lady's wear shop.

Leaning back on her sofa she smiled. Life was good. Purchasing Whimsical Woman had been one of the best things she'd ever done. Her move to Saltaire ran a close second.

She liked the temperate weather here, even the rainy days, plus the glorious landscaping and the relaxed and friendly people. Of course, during tourist season it wasn't always relaxed. But that was good because tourists helped pay her rent, wholesale costs, part-time salaries, and other expenses.

Carrying her half-filled wine glass, she returned to the kitchen. She hadn't thought about anything for dinner. She set the glass on the counter, opened the fridge, and stared at its contents. Before reaching a decision, she heard the phone ring. She walked across the room and picked it up. "Hello."

"Procne, this is Simon. I hate to be a nuisance, but is there any chance you could come over and help me again with Angelina?"

There goes dinner, she thought, and the rest of my Retsina. "Of course, Simon. What's the problem?"

"The same old thing. She's due back at Sunset Wing, and I can't get her moving."

Procne had no idea who had coined the name of the dementia wing in the hospital, but Sunset Wing seemed appropriate. "Does she want to stay at home?"

"I don't think she's even aware that she is at home. She just doesn't want to stand up and move."

"She's not aware she's at home?"

"No, she isn't."

"Does she know you?"

"I don't think so."

"Oh, Simon, how sad. Maybe there's not much point in bringing her home anymore."

"I'm starting to think that way, too."

"I'll hop in the car and be right over."

"Thanks, Procne. You're a godsend."

She drove her white Mazda from the parking garage and barely keeping within the speed limit reached Simon's two-story house. Parking at the curb, she considered phoning Brent if Angelina became too difficult. She jumped out of the car, dashed up the curving path to the front door, and rang the bell.

Simon promptly opened the door. "Procne, this is awfully good of you." His right hand tentatively touched her shoulder then quickly moved away. He stepped back and gestured for her to come inside.

She walked into the hallway, almost sorry that his hand hadn't lingered on her shoulder. Then she saw Angelina sitting in the armchair and reality came into focus. For many years Angelina and Simon had enjoyed a happy marriage and produced two good children. The ravages of time had been cruel to her, whereas Simon had developed into a healthy, vibrant, middle-aged man. But instead of enjoying the fruits of his life's work, he had spent much of his time and energy caring for a person who no longer knew he existed.

Now that Angelina was living in Sunset Wing, Simon no longer was responsible for her everyday needs. But Procne knew his love for her remained. Every so often, inklings of the woman she used to be shone through her mental fog. Unfortunately, those inklings were coming less and less often.

"She yells at me, kicks her feet, and waves her arms when I try to help her out of the chair."

"Oh, Simon. This is so hard for you." She took a deep breath and gingerly walked over to his wife's chair and squatted in front of her. "Hello, Angelina. I'm Procne." She saw the eyes stare blankly in her direction. "How are you feeling today?"

Angelina's eyes widened as if a light switch had been turned on and she politely replied, "I'm fine. How are you?"

"I'm fine, too. It's lovely outside. Would you like to go for a car ride?"

"That would be nice."

"I'll help you get out of your chair." Procne stood up, glanced at Simon who beamed appreciation to her. Then he went to Angelina's other side and together they hoisted her to her feet.

"What are you doing?" Angelina asked.

Procne thought her eyes looked frightened, so she kept her voice low-toned and soothing. "It's a lovely summer evening for a car ride." She saw Angelina's eyes go blank and felt her body succumb to gravity. Procne tightened her hold, afraid Angelina would collapse to the floor. The woman was heavy, a dead weight of about a hundred and thirty pounds. Thank goodness Simon strongly held her other side.

Between the two of them, they managed to get Angelina outside and into the front passenger seat of Simon's SUV. Simon closed the door and gazed at Procne.

"You were amazing. Thank you. I'll dash back and get her walker. Will you go to the Sunset Wing with us?"

"Yes, if you want me to."

"I do."

He dashed back to the house, returned with the walker, and put it in the trunk of his SUV.

At the hospital, Angelina ignored the walker so Simon dragged it behind him while he and Procne supported her between them. Once she tripped over nothing and they managed to keep her upright. Her feet again moved forward and her eyes stared at nothing in particular.

They carefully maneuvered her to the reception desk where the clerk stood up and said, "Good evening, Angelina."

Angelina paid her no attention. Simon and Procne slowly guided her into her room and helped her sit in her wheelchair. Simon pushed her to the window and she gazed out at the darkening world.

"Will the staff help her get ready for bed?" Procne asked.

"I could do it," Simon said, "but they're more adept than I am."

As if to prove his words, a nurse entered the room and asked Angelina if she had a nice time at home. Receiving no reply, the nurse turned to Simon and Procne. "I'll help Angelina put on her nightgown."

Simon kissed Angelina on the cheek. "Goodnight, dear heart. I'll see you tomorrow."

His wife gave no response, verbally or physically.

The nurse walked out of the room with them. "She is brightest in the morning. She loves looking out the window. Gradually, as the day goes on she becomes less alert. When she visits her home, does she know where she is?"

Simon shook his head. "She doesn't seem to. During her last two visits she didn't recognize anything. She just sits and gazes into space. I have trouble getting her to eat. She no longer knows that I'm her husband."

The nurse nodded sympathetically. "Maybe the time has come to forget about the trips home. They've become meaningless to her and hard on you and your daughter."

"Oh," Procne corrected, "I'm not his daughter, I'm just a family friend."

The nurse seemed a trifle flustered by her error, but covered it pleasantly. "Sorry. Her illness must be difficult for both of you."

"Yes," Simon admitted, "it is."

Outside, in the hospital parking lot, Procne climbed into the SUV and sat on the passenger seat Angelina had recently vacated. Simon drove and Procne watched the traffic which at this time of night was quite sparse. She noticed a car following a few car lengths behind them but paid little attention until it turned a corner after they did. Simon stopped in front of his house and the car sped up and quickly passed by them. It disappeared around another corner and Procne mentally shrugged. Who would have any reason to follow them?

"Have you had dinner?" Simon asked.

"No. I was thinking of putting something together when you phoned."

"I spent all my time trying to get Angelina to eat so ate nothing myself. I have some lasagna that I bought at the grocery store. I'll warm it up and we can toss a salad to go with it."

"Cool. Sounds better than I'd get at home."

He grinned and climbed out of the vehicle. She jumped to the street and they walked close together into the house. It all seemed perfectly natural.

Inside the kitchen, Simon took the lasagna from the fridge and popped it into the microwave. Procne cut lettuce, tomatoes, cucumber, and Walla-Walla sweet onion into a wooden bowl. With a wooden salad spoon and fork she tossed it. Simon set the table. He worked efficiently, having been chief cook and bottle washer long before Angelina went into Sunset Wing. He also was smart enough to eat healthily. They bumped into each other twice and laughed like teenagers.

Simon poured red wine into his stemmed glass. He held it over her empty glass and she held her hand over it. "Not for me. I have to drive home."

They sat down at the kitchen table and smiled at each other. Feeling surprisingly comfortable with him she started to eat.

Their conversation consisted mainly of food and what a boon for single people small, frozen meals had become. Then they discussed how Simon had started then managed the Historical Museum and how Procne managed Whimsical Woman.

Finally, as they finished their meal, Simon brought up the subject of his wife.

"I've finally faced up to the fact that Angelina is no longer with me and never will be again. Though the remnant of her body is here, her spirit has gone elsewhere." Simon sipped his wine and glanced around the room as if looking for the ghost of his wife. "I don't know where she is, but wherever it is, I hope she's happy there. I like living here in the town of Saltaire and I'm getting into the routine of living alone."

"Simon, you and Angelina were fortunate to have many happy years together. And you have two lovely children. Hang onto those memories." She hesitated a moment then said, "I had an unhappy marriage. But like you, I have two lovely children and I like living in Saltaire."

"You're already living alone and I, too, am more or less living without a spouse." He smiled wanly. "Procne, I appreciate your coming when I needed help."

"It was no problem." She felt a slight flush rise to her cheeks.

"I'm so wrapped up in my own life that I've never asked about yours. I know your divorce must have been traumatic."

"The trauma came before the divorce, Simon. The marriage was over long before I filed for divorce. We lived together until both our kids were almost through high school. The funny thing is that both Jane and Harold asked why it took me so long to divorce him. I've never badmouthed their father, but he said bad things about me, much of it exaggerated and some of it untrue. They felt the tension and saw and understood more than I realized. They still occasionally see him, but their attitude made the divorce easier for me. And of course I love Saltaire. I loved volunteering in the museum. And now I love working in my shop. I consider myself one of the luckiest people on earth."

Simon gazed at her. "Talk about positive thinking. I hope some of it brushes off on me."

She laughed.

They cleaned up the kitchen then Procne grabbed her purse and headed for the front door. He followed her and walked with her to the Mazda.

As she climbed into the driver's seat, he surprised her by saying, "In case that evil person is nearby, I'm going to follow you home."

"That's not necessary." She wondered who he meant by evil person. Had he noticed the car that seemed to follow them? "I'll keep my car doors locked until I'm in the townhouse garage."

"Do you have your cellphone with you?"

"Right here in my purse. It's handy. Surely you don't think the murderer will come after me."

"I just want you to be aware of the danger—just in case. After all, we don't know how many screws are loose inside his brain. Maybe a demon lives in there."

"That's pretty melodramatic." She closed the car door and opened the window. "At the hotel dining room last night, a few of us had a wake for Kathy and Annette. Some of us suspect the murderer has already left the island."

"I hope you're right." He leaned through the window and his lips touched hers. He stepped back quickly, obviously flustered. "I'll follow you. As soon as you're inside your home with the door locked, phone me."

"I will." To her own ears her voice sounded breathless. She, too, felt flustered. Easing the Mazda from the curb she realized her hands were trembling.

CHAPTER 31

Wednesday Evening, Continued

*H*e sat in his car and looked through his small binoculars. He saw the white Mazda go into the locked underground parking area and the dark blue SUV drive away.

With the help of the binoculars' magnification and the light of a nearby street standard he had watched the sinners go into Simon's house. When no one reappeared, anger had built within his body and bubbled into his thoughts.

Simon was betraying his wife. Procne, who pretended to be smart, was nothing but a home breaker. She apparently thought her beauty could entrap any man she wanted—out with one man last night and in the home of another tonight.

After returning from the hospital, why did she go into Simon's house? Why did she stay there for such a long time? What were they doing? Were their bodies pressed against each other and their legs entwined? He with a wife and both of them with children.

She ran a successful dress shop, but she needed to learn a lesson. She wasn't as perfect as she seemed to *think. The other two women learned their lessons the hard way. They, too, had been beautiful and successful. But at least they had no personal ties to a partner or to children. They could have obeyed his every word. But they didn't. They thought they were so clever, independent, and capable. Those three mistakes had been their downfall. They quickly learned that he was superior to them in every way. He was all powerful and they deserved their fate.*

Procne would learn that, too. And she would learn it very soon.

CHAPTER 32

Thursday Morning

Holding the phone to her ear, Philomela breathed a sigh of relief. "Procne, you're home. I phoned a few times last evening and there was no answer. Is everything okay?"

"Of course, Philomela. What could be wrong?"

"Well…nothing…I suppose." She refrained from mentioning the obvious—a murderer was on the loose.

"Simon called shortly after six last evening. He asked me to help take Angelina back to Sunset Wing. So, I did. Angelina's really out of it, Philomela. She doesn't know she's at home and she no longer recognizes Simon. It's so sad. A nurse at Sunset Wing even suggested that taking her home for visits was no longer beneficial, not for Angelina and certainly not for Simon."

"Does Angelina have any inkling of where she is?"

"None at all."

"Perhaps the nurse is right. What's the point of disrupting her and causing extra stress for Simon if it's of no value?"

"No point at all. Just a lot of trouble and heartache for no good reason. The nurse thought I was their daughter."

Philomela chuckled. "You look young enough. Angelina has aged physically as well as mentally, and Simon looks older because of the stress. However, Simon must have found the remark insulting."

"He didn't correct her. But I did. I explained I was a family friend. Anyway, the error didn't seem to bother him."

"He was probably too preoccupied with his wife and her illness to worry over such a minor thing."

"Maybe. I left my car at his place so he drove me back to it. He invited me to have dinner with him—warmed up lasagna. I made a salad."

"Nice."

"Yes, they were both good."

"I'm sure they were." She wondered if Philomela meant the food was good or the time with Simon was good. She didn't ask.

"When Simon walked me to my car, he insisted on following me home in his SUV. I told him that was unnecessary, but he insisted, even though I promised to keep the doors locked and keep my cellphone handy. He was afraid the murderer might attack me."

"Good for Simon. Until the murderer is caught, I think all women should take extra precautions. Realtors may not be his only target. By the way, did you enjoy dinner the other night with Roger and Melvin at the hotel?"

"Considering it was a mini-wake, we had a nice time. We eulogized the two victims and wished them bon voyage into their next life. The Trusts were there and a couple of other realtors. Jean Greenfield arrived in time for dessert."

"I know about Jean. Brent and I had lunch at the History Café yesterday and she told us she had arrived late. She thinks the murderer has left the island, but she admitted to having no facts to prove it. I suspect that's wishful thinking on her part."

"At the wake a few of us figured the murderer must have taken off. It would be too risky for him to stay here. Just in case, I hope the police are working day and night to find the culprit. Doubtless all the residents in Saltaire keep looking over their shoulders, expecting a tie to circle their neck."

"On a cheerier note, I had my hair trimmed at *Cut and Curl* yesterday afternoon."

"Who did it?"

"Sherry."

"Are you happy with the cut?"

"Yes, I like it. On a less cheery note, Sherry went to school with Annette. Collette, Sherry's partner, came back from a meeting with the police and she was awfully agitated. The police had asked her a lot of questions about Annette's sex life. All three of us expressed puzzlement as to why they would ask such questions. Collette suspects Annette was raped as well as being killed."

"Yuk. Not good. She figured that out on her own?"

"Yes."

'Maybe it's a good thing the police aren't giving out much information."

"Did Roger walk you home from the hotel dining room?"

"He and Sheila and Tom Trust. Roger wanted to have a nightcap at my place, but I begged off because it was late. Besides, I don't drink after dinner."

"Was he miffed when you rejected his suggestion?"

"He seemed to understand. But you know, something else occurred that was rather strange. Halfway through dinner at the hotel, I went to the necessary room. Melvin Springer followed me."

"Into the ladies' room?"

"No." Procne giggled. "He went to the Men's and I went to the Ladies'. But the strange thing was that he suggested we go on a picnic to Saltaire Island this Sunday. Just the two of us."

"What's strange about that?"

"Melvin isn't the picnic type. He likes shiny shoes and smart suits, not jeans, flip-flops or scruffy boots. When he and Maxine used to socialize, they always dressed to the nines and seldom ate at fast-food places. He made no bones about preferring to eat inside an attractive dining room than outside with ants and flies in a picnic area."

"Did you agree to go with him?"

"Well, sort of. He drank three or four Scotches, so he might forget that he asked me."

"Not likely."

"My kids are coming here in a couple of weeks. That leaves me free this Sunday to go with Melvin."

"Do you trust him?" Philomela asked.

"Trust Melvin? Of course, I trust him. Why wouldn't I trust him?"

"Circumstances. No other reason." Philomela knew she was grasping at straws that had no bearing on the case. Because Melvin's wife, Maxine, was murdered a year and a half ago didn't mean he had killed her. His good name shouldn't be dragged through the mud a second time. "I'm sorry I won't be here when Jane and Harold come to visit you."

"They'll be sorry to miss you, too. But once you move here permanently, you'll probably see more of them than you want."

"Never more than I want. I like my niece and nephew. They're good kids."

When her conversation with Procne ended, Philomela gazed out the window at her unkempt garden. Her thoughts, however, resided not on the garden but on her sister. She hadn't worried too much about Procne living alone before, but since the police still had no prime suspect, she was becoming paranoid. She wished she could watch out for her sister day and night. Naturally that was impossible. The one redeeming fact was that Procne and her neighbor, Selene, could keep an eye on each other. But they couldn't sit day and night on each other's doorstep.

Actually, the two murders were a frightening enigma. Was the perpetrator a local person with a personal grudge or a complete stranger who took advantage of opportunities as they arose? During the summer months the town was filled with tourists—boaters, tenters, motorhomers, relatives of residents, and travelers en-route to somewhere else. Anyone of them could have killed the two women. However, the killer could still be here, waiting to kill again.

She wondered if the murderer had known his victims. If so, the victims would have been at ease, not expecting an acquaintance or a friend to attack them. In that scenario the murderer would have had the advantage of surprise. After being without oxygen for a minute or so, the victim would be weakened. If rape as well as choking was an issue, then the perpetrator must have been a man. And a future victim would definitely be a woman.

Philomela's gut feeling leaned so strongly toward a male murderer that she decided not to waste time thinking of females who might be able to commit a murder. She would concentrate on males. If that took her to a dead end, then she would search a few different avenues.

She had been introduced by Procne to a lot of Saltaire residents, both male and female. She counted on her fingers those she had met who were of the male persuasion. Melvin Springer, Tom Trust, Roger Thistle, Simon Fraser, Hamish MacDonald, Corporal Stinson, Basil Devonshire. Seven men. Eight if she added her own dearly beloved—Brent.

Brent had been with her on the evening of Kathy's murder. Or had he? She tried to think back. They had tea with Kathy at the real estate office then returned to the motel. She had read her mystery novel while Brent went out to fill the truck with gas. Oh, oh—he had been gone a long while. There had been a long lineup of cars at the pumps. Was that important? She hoped not. She pushed it to the back of her mind by recalling that after he got back to the motel they had walked to the restaurant called, Fireside Pizza, and enjoyed dinner.

The afternoon Annette was killed Brent helped her clean their new house. Midafternoon, needing a pick-me-up, Brent drove his truck to Starbucks for two coffees. He was away for only a short time, certainly not long enough to drive to the crime scene. Or was it?

How could she even think of suspecting Brent? Was it because she wanted to immediately clear him of any suspicion? She knew he wasn't capable of murdering one person, let alone two, so what was wrong with her? Why was she wasting time and abstract thought in this manner?

She more or less struck Brent off her mental suspect list.

She should be trying to find other men who might be capable of doing the dastardly deed. The first step would be to glean information about the seven local men she had met.

How could she do that?

She didn't figure it out. Brent walked into the kitchen and disrupted her train of thought. She studied his face and asked, "Do you have any plans for today?"

"Nothing carved in stone. Is there anything special you want to do?"

"Not really. I was thinking I might read or check out some of the local shops."

"I might drive to the city of Victoria. I'd like to check out the ship chandler shops."

Philomela's eyebrows raised in puzzlement. "But you don't have a boat."

"That's immaterial. I understand those shops have a lot of neat things that might be useful around a house, especially a workshop."

She opened her mouth and closed it. Finally she opened it again. "Do we need more musty old stuff?"

He chuckled and shrugged his shoulders.

Oh well, she thought, if he enjoyed poking around funny old shops it would allow her time to do what she enjoyed—reading, checking out restaurants and shops, or compiling the idiosyncrasies of Saltaire's male residents.

"Do you want to join me?" he asked.

She shook her head. "It would be the reverse of you helping me look for a new dress."

"Not much fun."

Sitting on their lawn furniture in the dining room they sipped coffee and began to discuss what they should get rid of and how they should pack their remaining worldly goods for the big move to Saltaire. Various methods were hashed and rehashed and Brent finally stood up.

"When the time comes, we'll figure it out. I've dawdled long enough. I'm off to look at musty old stuff."

"See you later this afternoon."

CHAPTER 33

As she walked toward Main Avenue, Philomela heard footsteps behind her. She glanced over her shoulder and saw a husky young man a quarter of a block behind her. She slowed down but he seemed to maintain his original pace. She speeded up and so did he. His footsteps grew louder and faster. He was catching up to her. Should she run?

Suddenly the sound of footsteps ceased. Should she scream? Was he ready to grab her and swing a tie around her neck? Surely not in the middle of the day. She whirled around, bravely intending to face him.

She stared at the empty sidewalk. He was nowhere in sight. Then she saw him going up the steps of the house she had just passed.

Good grief. Her imagination was running wild. She must get a grip on herself. She was developing a case of perfect paranoia. Seeing a bit of humor in her over-wrought nervousness, she chuckled to herself and proceeded to walk briskly to Main Avenue. Instead of checking out other businesses, she went to Whimsical Woman.

She entered her sister's shop, heard the bell tingle, and noted a customer wearing a red coat browsing amongst a rack of winter and fall coats. The customer paid no attention to the bell, so intent was she in her search for the perfect garment. Philomela realized that for some people shopping could be very intense. She glanced at her sister and their eyes met. Standing behind the cash counter, Procne had apparently been doing paperwork.

"Hello, Philomela. What brings you here?"

"Your charming company, of course." Philomela briefly debated whether she should tell her sister about her recent, imaginative non-encounter. She decided to refrain—it was too silly and too embarrassing to mention.

"How about buying something? A pair of summer walking shorts? A sun dress? There are still a few on the sale rack."

"Not today. Today I want to pick your brains about a couple of people."

"Pick away."

Philomela glanced over at the customer who seemed oblivious of her. Gazing at her sister she asked in a sotto voice, "Do you think Melvin Springer could be capable of…you know…?" And she held her fingers and thumb around her neck.

"Oh, Philomela," Procne whispered. "Give it a rest. You're associating Melvin with these two new disasters simply because his wife had been stabbed a year and a half ago. He was proved innocent of Maxine's death, no ifs and no buts. I'm sure he's also innocent of these two recent ones."

"What about the rumors of his affair with Kathy? Could her rebuff have pushed him over the edge?"

"People have affairs all the time and they don't kill each other." Procne raised her voice. "What's wrong with you? Normally you don't give credence to rumors, not unless they are proved factual."

"You're right. I'm just trying to toss out the chaff while gleaning important information. Melvin's association with Kathy might be important."

The customer in the red coat left the coatrack and glided toward them. "I couldn't help overhearing," She looked accusingly at Philomela.

"Philomela," Procne hurriedly interjected. "This is Grace Devonshire. You met her last year."

"Of course. You're Basil's wife. You look wonderful, Grace." Philomela nervously recalled Grace's unhealthy addiction for shopping.

"Thank you." Grace raised her chin and looked down her nose at Philomela. "I think I should put you straight. Obviously you don't know that Basil and Melvin are good friends. My husband doesn't suspect Melvin of being involved with the deaths of the two young ladies. And yes, Melvin and Kathy saw a fair amount of each other. We even went out for dinner with them a couple of times. Melvin was starting to think of a long-term commitment, but Kathy was not prepared for an intimate relationship. As a result, she broke it off before anything too serious developed. Melvin was disappointed, but not overly so. He certainly wasn't upset enough to kill her."

"Thanks for setting me straight, Grace. I really don't want to harbor unwarranted suspicions." Philomela wondered if Grace had managed to overcome her addiction to buying things she didn't need and couldn't afford.

As if mind reading, Grace said, "You may recall my tendency to be a collector." Philomela nodded and Grace continued speaking. "Procne helps me quite a bit by suggesting I give a purchase more thought."

"Like a member of the Senate providing sober second thoughts to members of the House of Commons?" Philomela asked.

"I suppose you could describe it that way. Anyway, Procne always makes me stop and seriously think about something I'm tempted to buy. She asks why I want it, where and when I'll wear it. She even asks if I can afford it. She's lost quite a few sales by doing that."

"I'm glad to hear it, Grace." Philomela remembered how she had tried to curtail Grace's addiction by finger-pointing her as being a compulsive buyer. Trying to make Grace admit to her addiction, she had acted as bad cop while Selene Hamilton and Basil Devonshire had acted as good cops. They had rallied around Grace, supported and encouraged her to get help. Philomela later heard from Procne that Grace had joined Shopaholics Anonymous.

"To prove my renewed willpower," Grace said, "right now I'm going to leave the shop empty handed." She smiled at Procne and patted her arm. Then she returned her gaze to Philomela. "I can assure you that Melvin Springer is an upstanding citizen." She waved her hand and like a red sail in the sunset glided away.

"Well," Philomela said, "that was unexpected. But good for her. It seems Grace really does have a handle on her compulsive purchasing problem."

"She does, more or less. On the occasions when she does succumb, I remind her to keep the bill and return the item if she has any second thoughts about it. Twice she returned a couple of things and both times she had the bill. It was no problem for me."

"Well, she certainly didn't want me to think badly of Melvin."

Procne shook her head. "She told me she and Basil were supportive of Melvin in his new lifestyle. They helped him cope with being a widower. It's too bad things didn't work out for him and Kathy. Lately, he's been sniffing around me. I just hope he's not thinking of me as the next Mrs. Springer. I like him, but I don't want to marry him."

"Well, my dear, you are available." Philomela spoke like a wise old mentor. "You're also desirable. And you are a young, joyful divorcee. But right now, those qualities are not my concern. My concern centers on Melvin's capability of being the Saltaire strangler. According to Grace, he is an upstanding citizen. Didn't Jean Greenfield say Constable James mentioned a suspect as being upstanding? I won't worry about Melvin. But I do worry about you, Procne, especially after talking with Sherry and her hair-salon partner."

"I appreciate your concern, sis. If it will relieve your mind, I'll alert Selene. We can each watch for unwanted circumstances and undesirable men."

"Not just known undesirable men. Until the murderer is caught, keep a sharp eye on all men. Just in case." She smiled reassuringly. "But, for now, can I help you sell some summer stock?"

Procne shook her head. "At the moment I'm not busy. For most of the day things have been chugging along in an orderly manner. When autumn and winter stocks arrive, they keep me out of trouble. One of these days I might call on you to help me unpack and price garments."

Two customers entered the shop and Procne greeted them.

Philomela waved her fingers and took her leave. As far as a prime suspect was concerned, she was no wiser than when she had gotten out of bed this morning.

CHAPTER 34

Thursday Morning Later, Continued

S trolling along Main Avenue, Philomela saw two police officers walking half a block ahead of her. She quickened her pace and watched them enter the History Café. She nonchalantly followed them into the café and glanced around at the many coffee-break customers and a few late breakfast eaters. She watched Constable James stand at the counter and order while Corporal Stinson made his way to a small empty table butting against a wall and then sit down.

Easing behind the policewoman, Philomela watched her pay for and pick up two mugs of coffee. When she turned around Philomela smiled. "Hello, Constable James."

"Oh. Philomela. Hello."

"How is the investigation coming along?"

"Reasonably well. So, you and your husband really are moving to Saltaire."

"Yes. As you know, Annette Murphy showed us the almost perfect house. It was within our price range so we bought it.

"You told me you initially dealt with Kathy Holmes."

Philomela nodded. "A sad state of affairs. Two of our realtors were murdered."

"I knew both women quite well."

"Knowing a victim must make an investigation more difficult."

Looking downcast, the constable nodded. "It's hard to keep things from being colored with too much emotion."

"I'm sure that's true, especially if you liked the victims."

"And I did. Both of them."

"I liked them, too, though I knew them only briefly." Philomela stepped closer to the constable and lowered her voice to a whisper. "Yesterday I was at *Cut and Curl* when Collette returned after talking with you. From the questions she was asked she suspected rape had been involved."

The constable's eyes widened and for a second Philomela thought she would spill her coffee. "Oh my goodness. I suppose that was a natural assumption on her part."

"Was rape really involved?" Though she whispered, Philomela thought her question sounded blunter than she intended.

"In a manner of speaking. They occurred after death. We haven't made it public yet. But now…it seems a rumor has started, I guess we'll have to take that into consideration."

"Those insults occurred after death?" Philomela's tone of voice remained soft.

"The medical examiner thinks immediately after."

Philomela shuddered. The picture in her mind was becoming too graphic. "Do you think the victims suffered?"

"Not from the sexual assault. But of course the medical examiner says choking to death is an unpleasant way to die."

"Good grief. The perpetrator really must be mentally sick. Probably beyond redemption. I hope you catch him soon."

"I hope so, too. Already every female in town is on pins and needles."

"I know. I'm one of them."

Constable James briefly pursed her lips. "That's partly why we withhold a lot of information. Another reason is so we won't be inundated with crank calls from nutters who claim to having done the deed—They only want to see themselves in the newscasts." The constable's head moved slightly from side to side. "We're doing all we can."

"I'm sure you are."

As Constable James moved toward Corporal Stinson, Philomela stepped up to the counter and ordered coffee from Jean's assistant. After paying for it, Philomela looked around for a place to sit. The only empty chair she could see was at the table where the police sat. Should she join them? The idea of intruding on them made her feel tired, but she took a deep breath, picked up her coffee mug and strolled over to them. "Excuse me for interrupting."

The constable looked up at her and smiled.

"This is the only empty chair in the entire café. Would you mind if I joined you?"

"Please do, "Constable James said.

Corporal Stinson nodded politely, stood up, and pushed the empty chair from the table.

"Thank you." Philomela set her coffee on the table and sat down. After the corporal sat down again, she looked forthrightly at him and said, "Though curious, I hesitate to mention the ongoing enquiries. If you'd rather not talk about them, I understand."

"Everyone's talking about them, so I see no reason why you shouldn't." He took a sip of coffee.

Constable James explained to him that Philomela had talked with Collette yesterday. She quietly reiterated what the young girl had said upon her return from talking with the police.

Watching the corporal's reaction to the constable's words, Philomela thought he would make a good poker player. His facial expression didn't change. He appeared neither pleased nor displeased with the news.

"A logical assumption." He turned and briefly studied Philomela. "Do you know anything about the actual crimes?"

"Just that a man's tie was the murder weapon and what I gleaned from Collette's version of her interview with you. Constable James mentioned that being choked is an unpleasant way to die. Apparently, there was no rape…" Philomela glanced around at nearby customers.

Corporal Stinson nodded his head and softly said, "I'm not ready to let the press know about what happened after their deaths. Philomela, we'd appreciate your keeping this information to yourself, at least for a short while." He nonchalantly glanced to his side and behind. He seemed content that the other clients were too wrapped up in their own conversations to overhear his words.

"I'll zip my lips," Philomela promised.

"Have you heard any rumors or seen anything else that pertains to the two cases?" he asked.

"Not really. Most people hope the culprit is a stranger who has already fled the area."

"Possible but not probable," the corporal said.

"As an amateur sleuth, I think it's unlikely a woman committed the crimes." Unable to see how a female could physically rape a person, Philomela picked up her mug and took a quick sip of coffee. "I suppose you're check-ing all the males in Saltaire."

"All is a bit of an overstatement." The corporal smiled. "However, we are checking many of them. So far, most seem stalwart, upstanding citizens who were too busy with their own lives to commit any crimes."

Philomela took another sip of coffee, a longer one. It tasted good and seemed to revive her. "If a supposedly upstanding citizen did commit the crimes, how could an ordinary person help detect him as the murderer?"

"Good question. Many psychopaths are good at hold-ing their own in social situations—at least for a while. In fact, some of them talk so smoothly that most people have no inkling that they are manipulators, liars, cheats, and worse. Suspicions only arise after some of their handiwork is exposed. Then of course it's too late."

Philomela recalled what Grace had said about Melvin Springer. In Grace's eyes he was a perfect specimen of manhood. According to her, he hadn't been overly angry when Kathy dumped him. Selene had given Philomela a different impression. She studied Corporal Stinson and asked, "Has a psychologist come up with a personality picture?"

"Yes, but it isn't complete. Not yet."

"Will you be giving that information to the public?"

"Possibly. Later."

Their conversation veered away from the murders when Constable James asked Philomela about her new house. Philomela waxed happily about its good points. "I'm looking forward to becoming a Saltaire settler. But like everyone else, I'll be glad when you solve the mur-der."

After finishing their coffees, the three of them walked together from the café. There was no sign of the pollution warrior so Philomela asked if they knew the man.

"We do," Constable James replied. "So far, he's harmless. He has been treated for schizophrenia but often goes off his medication. Our concern is that someone will get him on illegal drugs. That will really knock him over the deep end."

"Could he be a murderer?" Philomela asked.

Constable James shook her head and Corporal Stinson said, "Unlikely, at this stage."

They bid adieu and went their separate directions.

Philomela thought about her chat with the police as she walked toward the sea-walk. Thanks to their conversation the after-death rape had been confirmed, but no other clues had come to the fore. Her pace slowed to a stroll and at a bench facing the Salish Sea, she sat down. Gazing at the water she let her thoughts flit back and forth. They finally centered on some of the men she knew here in Saltaire.

The pollution pontificator. The police said he was harmless. But could they be wrong?

Simon Fraser. He was busy with his job as curator of the museum and of course was wrapped up with his wife's rapidly increasing dementia. Could the unfairness of her life have unbalanced his mind? Could he have been angry because his once vibrant love was deteriorating before his eyes while women like Kathy and Annette had remained alert and sexy?

Melvin Springer. For a year and a half he had survived the murder of his wife. When Kathy rejected him, did he retaliate with uncontrollable anger, unknown to the Devonshires? Did he consider he had a right to kill Kathy?

Tom Trust. With Sheila so wrapped up in her classy shop, Upscale Garments, had he felt okay with having a brief affair with Kathy Holmes? And then did he kill her so she wouldn't tell his wife?

Roger Albert Thistle. Could he have been jealous of
the two female realtors? He seemed just as successful as
they were, so that idea might be a bit of stretch. But it
was worth looking into.

Hamish MacDonald. He was such a friendly person
and he loved his dog, Haggis. Could any dog lover con-
ceive of hurting another living being? She hoped not. But
then again, some people liked animals yet because of a
perceived insult could turn a human into an enemy.

Basil Devonshire. She knew from experience that under severe stress he could succumb to minor misdeeds
such as theft. He could also tell white lies if they protect-
ed someone he cared about. He was also quite enamored
with his own abilities so could be labeled as narcissistic.
But, she wondered, could he slip over the line into a psy-
chopathic state?

A narcissist likely wouldn't commit murder, but one
might cleverly manipulate someone else to commit a dastardly deed A psychopath was someone who suffered
from a mental disturbance that could end in unwarranted
violent behavior. Under normal circumstances that tendency might hide beneath wily charms and superficial
smiles.

CHAPTER 35

Sunday Morning and Early Afternoon.

Procne took more time with her make-up than usual. She fussed with skin cream, mascara and lip-stick—until she realized how silly it was. Why try to be a prima donna, especially at a casual picnic? If she ended up swimming in the salt-chuck, her facial art, no matter how skillfully applied, would be gone in a second.

What was she thinking? With her dark eyebrows and lashes she didn't need mascara and her skin was still quite unblemished. Gazing at her reflection she saw tiny crowfeet forming at the corner of her eyes, but they weren't very noticeable. She shrugged and thought: Middle age approaches. So what? She certainly had no intention of trying to impress or seduce Melvin Springer. He had good qualities, but she felt no attraction to him, not physical or emotional or mental.

She turned from the mirror, took her bikini from the chest of drawers, put it on her naked body and covered the tiny garments with a sundress. She dropped a clean bra and panties in her beach bag and tucked in some money in case she needed an emergency ferry ride home. That was that. She was ready for anything.

Melvin had said he would pick up lunch from Jean Greenfield. All she had to do was come herself and bring water and a thermos of coffee. She couldn't remember if fresh water was available on the small island, so she filled her old water bottle with tap water. A plumber once told her that tests had proved the local tap water was better than all the bottled waters sold in stores. She dropped the bottle and thermos in with her clean underclothes and mad money.

Carrying the beach bag, she sauntered through the open-air vestibule and out the metal gate. She glanced down at the interlocking red bricks then watched vehicles zoom along the street and disappear from sight. She stood near the curb and saw Melvin's black Range Rover glide over the pavement and stop beside her. She opened the door and climbed into the passenger seat.

"Good morning," he said. "A lovely day for a picnic."

"Couldn't be better. You survived the mini-wake okay?"

"I did. But I still can't believe those two young women are gone."

"Me neither. It's sad and scary. Like all the women in town, I hope the police find the killer soon."

He concentrated on driving and said nothing more until he parked near the small ferry dock. He started to buy two ferry tickets, and when Procne tried to intercept and buy her own, he said, "My treat."

The sixteen-passenger ferry was at the dock. The tide was out so the ramp was steep. After a six-minute ferry ride they climbed onto the exceedingly wide beach of Saltaire Island, the island that took its name from the nearby town.

Melvin carried his picnic bag and she carried her smaller beach bag. Side by side they made their way along the sandy beach. Already large and small groups had claimed personal territories with towels, sun umbrellas, and folding chairs. Procne knew some of them would be forced to move their paraphernalia back from the water when the tide flowed in, but that wouldn't happen for a few hours. Motor yachts and sailboats tied to buoys or anchored nearby bobbed in the gentle waves. They would be unaffected by the incoming higher water.

Procne scanned the lengthy stretch of beach. "Let's wander along the sand and find a tidal pool. Watching the tiny creatures swimming in them is always interesting."

The tidal pool they selected was about eight feet across and seemed four or five feet deep. They knelt on their knees, leaned forward, and gazed at minnows and other tiny sea creatures. The miniature swimmers ignored the two human beings and their moving shadows.

After arranging their paraphernalia on the sand near the tidal pool, they sat down and watched some young children run back and forth. Procne eventually asked, "Should we go for a swim in the salt-chuck?"

"Let's eat first. I didn't have much breakfast so I'm hungry."

Melvin opened his picnic bag and Procne was amazed at how much it held—

tablecloth, serviettes, two plates, two stem glasses, cutlery, bottle of non-alcoholic elderberry wine, and food in the form of fried chicken, salads, and buns.

"This is a feast," she said. "You and Jean Greenfield outdid yourselves."

"Only the best for the best shop-owner in town."

She giggled. "I wish."

With a flourish he opened the bottle of elderberry wine, filled a glass, and handed it to her. Then he filled the second glass for himself. "To us." He clinked his glass against hers and took a lengthy sip.

His "to us" made her slightly nervous. What exactly did he mean? She was afraid to ask.

Melvin leaned back and sighed. "This is the life. Just think, when we retire, we could do this every day of the week."

"If we picnicked every day of the week it would become humdrum. Not a special treat."

"You're right." He shifted position and abruptly changed the subject. "Have you ever thought about marrying again?"

The question caught her off guard. In fact, it stunned her. She swallowed then managed to reply with total honesty. "Melvin, my marriage was a disaster. If it hadn't been for our two children, we would have divorced years ago. As a result, I have no wish to try that institution again. I'm happy being single and happy managing my own business."

"Maxine and I had a lot of good times together. I'd like to marry again. Needless to say, I've known you for a few years and am very fond of you."

"Don't go there, Melvin." Seeing disappointment flood his face, she softened her words by saying, "I'm fond of you. But at this point in time, I'm not interested in a close relationship with anyone. Not with you or anyone else."

For a minute they sipped their elderberry and gazed at everything except each other. Then Melvin brought out the fried chicken and said, "There's no reason we can't enjoy the food."

They enjoyed every mouthful of the entire lunch.

"My mother would never let us go in swimming right after eating," Procne said. "She insisted we wait at least an hour to prevent the possibility of getting stomach cramps. I haven't always abided by that rule, and, so far, I've never developed cramps."

"I know that rule, too. Like you, I've never been troubled with cramps after swimming too soon after eating."

"Do you think we could have a dip now?"

"I don't know why not." He stood up and stripped off his shirt and shorts.

Procne was relieved to see he wore swimming trunks. They were dark gray in color and accentuated his slim hips. Hearing a few squawks, she glanced past him.

"Oh, look. A murder of black crows is strutting on the sand."

He looked and laughed. "Why is it a murder of crows instead of a flock of crows?"

"I don't know. It's a silly expression, isn't it." The silliness of murder faded as thoughts of Kathy and Annette filled her mind.

A few minutes later, Procne and Melvin ignored the crows and ran like teenagers across the beach to the saltchuck. After the first shock of cold water hit Procne's abdomen, she dived headfirst into the deepening water. She extended her arms at each side of her head and did her version of the Australian crawl. It wasn't a great stroke, but it was relatively smooth and moved her parallel with the shore. She gave her arms, legs, and lungs a good workout. Feeling invigorated she turned and swam back parallel with the shore. With her face in the water, she saw Melvin's gray trunks shimmer near her.

Something banged the back of her head. She felt stunned. Stars danced within her eyes and she sputtered and coughed. She tried to stand up but was unable to touch bottom so had to tread water. She flapped toward shore and tried again to stand up. Her right foot slipped on a rough stone. She swam a few more strokes, tried again to stand, and this time her feet landed on smooth, firm sand. She took a couple of deep breaths and looked around her, hoping to see what had hit her head. No boat

and no swimmers were nearby. On the beach three children stood listening to a woman who seemed to be lectur-
ing them. A few feet away from her Melvin's feet
splashed, propelling his body toward shore.

Apparently, he had not seen anything untoward. She
wondered if his foot could have accidently hit her head.
Could the rough rock she stepped on somehow have
banged her head? Could a meteorite have fallen from the
sky?

Her fingers touched the back of her head which was
wet—doubtless from the saltwater. She lowered her hand
and was surprised to see not colorless water but a sticky
redness. She touched her head again, lowered her hand,
and studied her red fingers. Blood. She was bleeding.

She stood up and waded toward shore. Melvin walked
in the water ahead of her and as he left the salt-chuck he
didn't glance back, not until he was well up on the beach.
When he turned around and saw her, she saw no expression of concern on his face. He stood motionless and
waited for her to approach him.

"Did you enjoy your swim?" he asked.

"I did. But something hit my head. Maybe a seagull or
a crow dropped a seashell or something. I'm bleeding."

He came up to her and studied the back of her head.
"My god, Procne, you really are bleeding. We should get
you to the hospital."

"Head's bleed easily. I wasn't even knocked out." At
least she was pretty sure she hadn't been knocked out.

"Procne, this could be serious. You could have con-
cussion."

"Don't fuss, Melvin. I appreciate your concern, but
I'm okay."

They walked farther up the beach and Melvin took
hold of her arm. But instead of helping her he seemed to

lean on her, making her wish he would let go and allow her to walk on her own.

She glanced over at the three children. The woman still talked sternly to them. Was she scolding them for throwing stones into the water? Could one of their stones have hit her head?

Near the tidal-pool, Procne sat on the sand. "I'm going to rest for a few minutes." She lay down on her side and stretched out her body, keeping the injured area free of sand by resting her head on her beach bag.

Melvin fussed over her and put a towel on top of the beach bag under her head. He finally lay down beside her. "I still think you should go to emergency."

"It doesn't hurt." She rested her fingers on her head and felt the formation of a bump. She closed her eyes.

They relaxed in the sunshine until their swimsuits were almost dry. Finally, she stood up and slipped her sundress over her head. She discreetly replaced her bikini top with her clean bra. After the sundress fell over her thighs, she deftly replaced her bikini bottom with her panties. She felt like a magician replacing a handkerchief with a dove.

Melvin rose to his feet, slipped into his shirt and put his shorts on over his swimming trunks. They picked up their gear, walked side by side and again he took her arm. This time he offered real support. He frequently checked her head to see if it had stopped bleeding. It had.

After the short ferry ride to town, they stepped onto the ramp. The tide had flowed in enough to make the ramp almost horizontal so walking on it required no extra effort. They strolled on the road to Melvin's Range Rover and he drove her home, fussing every so often about her injury. He walked to the townhouse with her and waited while she unlocked the door.

"I'm okay, Melvin. You don't need to worry about me anymore"

"I should come in with you."

The last thing in the world she wanted was for him to come inside. "Honestly, Melvin, I'm fine. I promise to put some ice on my head and lie down for a short while."

"I could make you a cup of tea or something. You shouldn't be left alone."

"I feel fine. The outing was great fun…until my stupid accident. Thanks for a lovely day, Melvin. See you soon. Bye for now. And thanks again."

She stepped inside and partially closed the door. Saying goodbye a second time she shut the door firmly.

As much as she liked Melvin, she felt at ease now he was gone. In the bathroom she emptied her beach bag, rinsed saltwater from her bikini, and hung it over a towel rack to dry. She held up a hand mirror and studied the back of her head. With a clean, moist washcloth she dabbed off the dried blood and applied some hydrogen peroxide. In the hand mirror she could see it fizz. Then she went to the kitchen and from the freezer extracted a small package of frozen corn, wrapped a dishtowel around it and placed it on the lump that had formed on her head. She recalled a chiropractor once advising her to use frozen corn rather than frozen peas as an ice pack. His theory was that peas become mushy faster than corn.

Then she remembered her front door. She hadn't locked it. She strolled over to it, clicked the lock, and returned to the sitting area. She lay down on a sofa and held her improvised icepack against the swelling on her head.

She recalled the initial bang on her head. Whatever hit her must have been quite hard because it broke her skin and the lump it created was a fair size. The contents of a seagull's intestinal tract wouldn't have done that. Besides, no white spatter had hit her head and shoulders. She wondered if a crow or a seagull really had dropped a seashell. She thought with little credence that a meteorite had fallen from the sky.

Then she remembered stepping on what felt like a rough stone on the sea bottom. Could someone have thrown it? Were the three children on the beach big enough to heave a stone that far?

She should have asked Melvin what he thought might have hit her.

Perhaps not. He was swimming near her when the object slammed against her head. Could he have thrown a stone at her?

She was being stupid. Melvin was not vindictive. One minute he wanted to marry her and the next minute he wanted to injure or kill her? It was too ridiculous to contemplate.

Then again, because of the two murders, Philomela had told her to be careful of all men, even those she knew and liked. Her older sister sometimes saw shadows that didn't exist, but not often. And Procne had to admit her sister knew quite a bit about murder.

CHAPTER 36

Sunday Afternoon

Philomela picked up the phone, read the call display, and clicked talk. "Hi, sis. Are you home from your picnic with Melvin?"

"I am."

"Did you have a nice time?"

"Yes…until I got hit on the head."

"What?"

Procne explained what had happened while she was swimming in the salt-chuck.

"Good grief. Has it quit bleeding?"

"Yes. I wasn't knocked unconscious."

"Thank goodness for that. You have no idea what hit you or who instigated the action?"

"No. I stepped on a stone lying on the sea bottom. It seemed out of place so it might have been the guilty instrument. Children on the beach were tossing stones so they could have tossed one my way. Then again, it might have been a meteorite." She laughed. "Or Melvin could have hit me."

"Why would he do that?"

"No reason. I really don't think he did it."

"Any other explanations?"

"Not that I can think of."

"Any boats near you?"

"None."

"If it was a meteorite or a child's stone there's not much you can do about it. One of the children tossing a stone seems the most logical, especially since you saw the mother reprimanding them. However, I suggest you avoid being alone with Melvin—to be on the safe side. At least until the murderer is caught."

"Okay. I think he wants to get married again."

"To you?"

"Maybe."

"Well, he has an eye for stunning women. Perhaps he just wants arm candy."

Procne giggled. "Maybe."

"Do you want me to come over?"

"No. I have a bump on my head, but I'm fine. Gosh, I'll be glad when the murderer is caught."

"Me too. So will everyone. If Brent and I go for a walk later on, we'll pop in and see you."

"Okay. I'll be here all evening."

Philomela went out to the back yard where Brent was setting up the sun dial he had bought at the ship chandler shop. He paused and stared at it.

"Are you having a big think?" she asked.

He turned and grinned at her. "Yes, I was thinking about the best way to install it. I think I've figured it out."

"Good. Procne just phoned." She told him about the picnic on Saltaire Island.

"Why would Melvin hit her on the head?"

"She doesn't think he did. He was solicitous, even offered to take her to the hospital."

"She doesn't know what hit her?" He glanced at the

sundial as if it might provide an explanation to why Procne was hit on the head.

Philomela suspected he found the installation of the sundial more interesting than the lump on Procne's head, so she turned to go back in the house. A movement next door caught her eye. Mary Skidmore stepped outside and waved at her.

"Hello, Philomela. I've just made a fresh pot of coffee. Would you and Brent like a cup?"

"Not me, thanks," Brent said. "I want to finish this sundial."

Philomela accepted the invitation and as she entered Mary's yard her hostess directed her to the patio. Philomela sat down at a table under a bright umbrella and admired Mary's garden. The woman obviously had a green thumb. A raised bed held carrots, peas, and cucumbers. Shrubs and flowers surrounded a lawn and Philomela recognized some shrubs because they still had a few blueberries on their branches. The berries looked plump and juicy.

Mary saw her looking at the bushes. "Strawberry and raspberry seasons are over, but I still have a few blueberries and blackberries." She set a tray with muffins, cream, sugar, and two mugs of steaming coffee on the table. "Would you like a blueberry muffin?"

"They look delicious. But Brent and I ate a short while ago. Besides, if I don't watch my figure, no one else will."

"You don't have to worry about that. But then again, lots of people like watching fat people."

"Yes, they can be fascinating." Philomela sipped her coffee. "According to what I heard on the radio yesterday, the Middle-east and Africa have the most obese people in the world. You'll never guess what western country has the biggest percentage of obese people."

"The USA?"

"No. The UK."

"That surprises me," Mary said. "I was in Las Vegas a couple of years ago and obese people were everywhere. Very different to what I remember sixty years ago. During World War Two, food rationing and lack of petrol helped keep everyone slender and very fit."

Philomela looked with surprise at her neighbor. "Are you old enough to actually remember the war years?"

"Indeed. I'm eighty-eight."

"Good grief. You don't look it."

"Thank you. You say all the right things." Mary chuckled.

Philomela gazed at her neighbor's white hair and few facial wrinkles and realized how her slim figure and youthful agility minimized those aging signs. "I thought you were in your early seventies."

"Thank you. Good Norwegian genes and a well-balanced diet help. I also get lots of exercise doing my own housework. When working in the garden I always wear a brimmed hat."

"Do you take vitamin supplements?"

Mary nodded. "In 1950, my nursing nutrition text was published before antibiotics became rampant, so vitamins filled one long chapter. I've learned more since, of course, but I don't worry if I miss a day here or there. The supplements seem to help me, but my husband was not so fortunate. He died of a heart attack a few years ago."

"I'm sorry."

"I still miss him. But it was better than a lingering death with Alzheimer's disease."

Philomela nodded. "I know a lady who has early onset Alzheimer's. Simon Fraser's wife."

"Yes, I met her several years ago. She's a lovely person. Too young to have Alzheimer's."

Philomela knew Angelina was in her late fifties which, to a woman in her mid- fifties, was still middle age. Mary, however, classified the late fifties as young.

"It's hard on the family. How is Simon doing?"

"He's coping. Angelina is in a care facility now. Apparently, she doesn't always recognize him. Procne sometimes helps him."

"Procne? You mean the new owner of Whimsical Woman?"

"Yes. She's my sister."

"Incredible. You and she are so dissimilar in appearance. She seems to be doing a good job with the shop. Maxine Springer's death was a dreadful tragedy. She and I used to be on the board of the Historical Museum. She was a real spark plug. I confess to sometimes thinking her husband is an odd duck."

Philomela smiled. "He seems to be looking for someone to replace Maxine. Yesterday he took Procne for a picnic on Saltaire Island."

Mary gazed steadily at Philomela. "Apparently Melvin had nothing to do with his wife's death. But for some reason I never really cottoned on to him."

Philomela leaned toward her neighbor. "Do you know why?"

"Probably just personality quirks."

"Do you think Melvin's capable of murder?"

"Murder? I doubt it. Is your sister romantically interested in him?"

"She considers him a friend, that's all."

"I'll get more coffee." Mary stood up and took both mugs into the kitchen. She returned and set two steaming mugs on the table.

Philomela stared longingly at the blueberry muffins. "Do I really care if no one else watches my figure? No."

She picked up a muffin and took a bite. "Mmm. Good."

Mary chuckled and took a muffin herself. "I've lived in this town all my married life. I used to know just about everybody. But not anymore. The town is growing by leaps and bounds. I can't believe all the condominiums that are being built."

Philomela chewed and swallowed. "It's called progress. Do you know Sheila and Tom Trust?"

"Yes. Tom started his real estate firm about twelve years ago and has done very well. He seems easy going, but maybe that's because Sheila is so energetic, always busy doing something, whether it needs doing or not."

Philomela wondered if Mary had heard the gossip about Kathy Holmes and Tom. She thought not, so refrained from repeating it. Instead she said, "When I was here a year and a half ago, I got to know Basil and Grace Devonshire quite well."

"A lovely couple. Grace is a great shopper, but she clings to the past. I understand she never throws anything out. Jim used to tell me that when I bought something new I must either give something to the thrift shop or throw something out. Grace doesn't abide by that rule." She closed her eyes as if hearing her husband's voice. Opening them she said, "That rule, I'm afraid, is easier said than done."

Philomela nodded agreement. "I knew Grace was a shopaholic, but I hadn't thought of her as being a hoarder. Then again, I suppose the two traits do meld together."

"They can go hand in hand." Mary held up both hands with palms facing Philomela. "I don't mean to gossip, because Grace may have overcome those tendencies. I haven't been in their house for several years."

"I've never been in it." Philomela recalled how Basil had coped with a wife who spent as if there were no tomorrow. And now she learned the woman was a hoarder to boot. Philomela couldn't imagine living in a house jammed to the rafters with stuff. She pressed her lips together and then turned to a cheerier subject.

"Mary, after I get serious about our garden, I'll come to you for advice."

"Any time."

When Philomela returned home and entered the front hall, she gazed at Brent, shocked. He was standing beside his overnight bag. Her heart sank. What was going on?

"Philomela, I just got a call from southeast Saskatchewan. A well there is having problems. I know I can fix it. I've got a return airline ticket to Regina and have rented a car to drive to the field. My flight leaves in an hour and a half. Will you be okay?"

"Of course." She didn't mention that she'd be a single woman alone in their house with a murderer on the loose. His job was important, and he was good at solving problems. She smiled. "How long will you be away?"

"I should get back in a few days. I was lucky to get on this flight. Will you drive me to the airport?"

She nodded.

At the airport, Brent parked his truck in front of the departure area. They both jumped out and he grabbed his overnight bag. Standing on the sidewalk, she gave him a tight hug and a lingering kiss on the lips. Then she watched him walk toward the open door of the terminal.

CHAPTER 37

Sunday Evening

A white car pulled up behind the truck, and Philomela saw Tom Trust jump from the driver's side. He hurried to the trunk of his car, brought two suitcases to the passenger side of his vehicle, and set them on the sidewalk. As he opened the passenger door, he noticed Philomela and waved.

She returned his wave just as an elegant lady stepped from the car. A tall man followed her and they each shook hands with Tom then grasped the handles of their suitcases. They pulled their bags to the entrance of the terminal, and Tom walked over to Philomela.

"What brings you here?" he asked.

"I brought Brent to the airport."

"Oh, so, you're alone."

"Just for a day or two. Brent's off to Saskatchewan to solve a problem. Why are you here?"

"I delivered two clients who bought a condominium. They're going home to Montreal and will return for the final closing at the end of November."

"Will they live here permanently?"

"Eventually."

"Well, I mustn't take up the departure parking space any longer. See you around, Tom."

"You bet."

She climbed into the driver's seat of the truck and shoulder checked. Seeing no oncoming vehicle, she eased the truck from the curb and drove away. But she didn't go home.

Instead she went to the hospital, intending to check out Angelina's reference to a hole in the ground. She parked in the parking lot, got a ticket from the machine, and placed it on the dashboard. After walking around the Sunset Wing, she entered the lawn between it and another wing. The landscaping was pretty but simple—the smooth lawn was bordered with shrubs and flowers. She saw Angelina sitting in her wheelchair looking out the window. Philomela waved, but Angelina did not respond.

Keeping the patient's line of vision in mind, Philomela walked along the shrub and flower bed of the other wing. She was rewarded with a hole in the colorful bed. It looked as if a gardener had taken out a dead shrub but forgot to put in a new, healthy one. There was no sign of a body and nothing else looked remotely suspicious.

She waved again at Angelina, who again did not respond, then made her way around the Sunset Wing back to her car. As she drove from the parking lot, she glimpsed a white car pulling out of its parking space. She saw it behind her but paid it no attention until she turned into her driveway. It zoomed along the road behind her and disappeared.

Strange, she thought, the car resembled Tom Trust's Cadillac.

After putting the truck in the garage, she went in the house and walked to the living room. She reached up to close a blind and through the window noticed the same white car move slowly along the road. As it passed by her house, she recognized the driver.

What was he doing here? Was he stalking her? Did he see her looking at him?

She hurriedly pulled down the blind.

She stood beside the window for a few seconds then dashed around the house making sure all the outside doors were locked and the chain hooked on the front door. She ran downstairs. The basement windows were big enough for a slim person to squeeze through so she closed them tightly. As she climbed up the stairs the front doorbell rang.

She froze. "Good grief. Who is it?" She tip-toed to the door and peered through the peephole.

With a thumping in her chest, she opened the door but kept the chain in place. "Hello, Tom. What are you doing here?"

"Checking on you. Is everything all right?"

"Everything's fine."

"Do you want me to come in and look around the basement for you?"

"No need. I've already done it. But thanks for offering."

"You're sure I can't be of help?"

"I'm sure."

"Well, I'll leave you then." He stood still and looked at the chain.

"Thanks again, Tom. See you around." She closed the door and flicked the lock. With heart still banging loudly in her chest, she peered through the peephole and watched him go down the front path to his car.

In the living room, she peeked through a space between the blind and the window frame and watched him drive away. In the dining room, she sighed and collapsed on a patio chair. She sat there like a zombie until her heartbeat returned to normal.

Before getting ready for bed, she leaned a broom against the wall near the bed and placed her car remote and her cellphone on Brent's pillow.

Tonight might be—Sleepless in Olympus.

CHAPTER 38

Monday Morning

Philomela awoke with surprise and looked at her wristwatch. She had slept soundly for more than seven hours. She reprimanded herself for not tossing and turning with nervousness—she was supposed to be in terror of a murderer. Remembering Procne, Selene, and her neighbor Mary, she forgave herself. Saltaire was home to many widows, divorcees, and other single females who seemed not to suffer from sleeplessness.

The murderer would have no interest in her or Mary Skidmore—too old. But who knew? She thought of her rude behavior last night to Tom Trust, not even inviting him inside. He said he was checking things out for her, and he probably was.

Or was he?

She was becoming paranoid. She hated to think how realtors and younger women were coping. Some of them must be absolutely petrified with fear.

When she and Brent left the island to prepare for the big move to Saltaire, she would worry about her kid sister living alone. It was an unappealing prospect. Her imagination already visualized horrid scenes. Everyone knew the murderer might attack again. But nobody knew who he'd choose next. So far, of course, the killer's prime targets had been young, single, female realtors who had graduated from the same high school.

Right now, she had a wish list that consisted of one thing—find the perpetrator. She would do her utmost to find him. To obtain his identity she must put forth more effort.

She looked out the window at the sundial and thought of Brent. He had set it up yesterday near the patio. Before doing so, he had sat on a patio chair supposedly reading his adventure novel though his book had fallen on his chest and his breathing had grown slower and deeper. This was happening more and more often. Time and increasing age were taking their toll. In four months he would be sixty-three. Though still physically active, agile, and alert, he tired more easily. His stamina and recuperative powers were less than they were a few years ago. It truly was time for him to think of retirement—at least of semi-retirement.

And yes, she had to admit, she was not that many years behind him—six to be exact. Procne, of course, was still a kid, ten years younger than her older sister.

Philomela wanted to use her energy and observational skills to snoop around for murder clues. The question was—where should she start?

Men's wear shops? Coffee shops? Barber shops? No, the best place to start would be the Historical Museum.

On Main Avenue she walked down the exterior stairs and entered the museum. For a town the size of Saltaire, the museum was more than adequate and thanks to Simon Fraser it was extremely well run. Items were cleverly displayed, and volunteers generously donated their time, skills, and money. Procne had enjoyed working there before buying Whimsical Woman. Now, running the ladies-wear shop took up most of her time. It was employment she really enjoyed.

Inside the museum, Philomela was greeted with the familiar Scottish burr. "Good morning, Philomela."

She smiled at the man sitting on a high stool behind the counter. "Good morning, Hamish. How are you and Haggis today?"

"I'm fine and Haggis is asleep on his cushion beside me. Do you want to tourrr the museum?"

"Another time, Hamish. Right now, I want to talk with you about the two murders."

"Ach. Terrrible, terrrible. Two such lovely lassies."

"Yes, the murderer targets attractive, single women."

"That he does."

"Your observing eyes helped solve Maxine Springer's murder. I thought you might have observed something that would help solve this one."

"Sorrry, Philomela, I have seen nothing suspicious."

"Hamish, apparently something happened that has cut the suspect list in half. Only the male half is under specific suspicion."

"Should I be flatterrred that you considerr me a suspect?"

She chuckled. "To be honest, I don't consider you a suspect. I consider you a good detector. Would you keep me up to date with anything you consider weird or unusual?"

"Aye. Give me yourr phone numberr, lass, and I'll do what I can."

She gave him her business card with her cellphone number on it. Then she asked, "How do you think Simon is managing?"

"He wasn't good for a long time. Howeverr, this past week he finally seems to be accepting Angelina's fate. I think he felt life was being unfair—she's so ill and he's so healthy."

"It's called survivor guilt."

"Yes, that descrribes it. He's grradually rrenewing his enerrgy and again using his skills at the museum."

"That's good." She wondered if Simon's renewed energy had anything to do with the deaths of the two singe women. Oh dear, was she unintentionally accusing him? Not really, and she mentally slapped her wrist for the unkind thought. More likely it was Procne's cheery friendliness that was helping him cope. "What about Basil Devonshire?"

"Basil was in good spirits...until he learrned of Kathy's death. He knew herr quite well. I believe he and Grrace sometimes went out for dinner with Melvin Springerr and Kathy. You might ask Basil if he has any suspects in mind."

"Will Basil be closing the museum this afternoon?"

Hamish nodded. "Aye."

"Thanks for chatting with me, Hamish. I'll keep in touch. Did you know Brent and I will soon be moving here?"

"I hearrd you bought a house. It will be Calgarry's loss and Saltairre's gain."

She smiled. "Thanks, Hamish. You're very kind."

With an airy wave she walked through the open doorway, went upstairs to Main Avenue, and turned into the History Café. She hoped Jean Greenfield might have gleaned news regarding the apprehension of the murderer.

CHAPTER 39

Monday, Late Afternoon

Preparing to close the shop for the day, Procne was surprised to see Roger Thistle walk through the open doorway.

"Hi, good looking. How are you this dreary Monday?"

She laughed. "Hello, Roger. It's not dreary. The sky is blue and the sun is just starting to set."

"Okay, it's a nice fall day."

"How are things at Trust Realty?" His pale blue eyes reminded her of winter rather than of autumn, but he looked smart in his shirt, tie, and gray suit.

"The office is slowly getting back to normal."

"I bet the female realtors haven't overcome their fear of a serial killer."

"Well, there's only Myrtle left. She spends a lot of time lamenting the absence of the two young girls. She's getting to be a pain in the neck."

"She must miss them. And she must be nervous about the killer targeting females."

"Young females. Myrtle is sixty-five years old. Why would anyone go after her?"

Procne shrugged. "I don't know."

"Life and sales go on."

"I suppose they do."

"How are Philomela and Brent? I think the house they bought is a disaster."

"Not really. It just needed a good cleaning. The place suits them—not too big, not too small. Actually, the house is cute and has a nice floor plan. The garden will be lovely after it's given a lot of tender loving care."

"Will Brent semi-retire?"

"That's the plan."

"Procne, I know you're busy, but how about having dinner with me one of these days? I miss Kathy and Annette. A bit of female companionship would be nice."

She had been surprised when Roger wanted to take her to the mini-wake, now she was surprised at his offer to take her out for dinner. But she admitted to herself that the invitation was flattering. He was good looking and when he wanted to be, he was quite charming. "I'd like that."

"Tonight? Tomorrow? The next day?"

Procne chuckled. "As a matter of fact, I'll be free today as soon as I close the shop."

"Excellent. Do you have a favorite restaurant?"

"Not really. I enjoy other people's cooking, no matter where it is."

"Why don't I pick you up at your place in an hour? Would that be okay?"

"Perfect. That'll give me time to try and make myself beautiful." She grinned.

"You don't need time; you look beautiful right now."

Feeling flustered, she giggled, "Thank you very much."

"See you in an hour." He turned and strode out of the shop.

At home, she quickly showered, put on a dash of lip-stick, and combed her hair. She slipped into a filmy summer dress, studied it in her full-length mirror, and hoped it would serve as a model for the sale of similar ones in the shop.

Outside, she shifted her weight from one high-heeled sandaled foot to the other. She waited on the sidewalk partly because the evening was lovely and partly to avoid inviting Roger into her home. Silly of her, but she took Philomela's warning advice to heart—Do not trust any man until the killer is caught. Could the handsome and charming Roger Thistle be capable of something sinister—date-rape or putting an end to someone's life?

The recent murders hadn't made her completely paranoid, but she had no intention of letting her guard down. She accepted the idea that caution is the better part of valor.

Roger drove up in his sleek gray car and stopped at the curb. He jumped out, strode to the passenger side, and the opened door.

She flirtatiously batted her eyelashes at him. "Such gallantry."

"A classy new restaurant opened recently not far from the ferry terminal. It's called Sea Breeze Place."

"I've heard of it. Apparently, it has white tablecloths and everything." She was pleased that her dress and sandals would be appropriate for the semi-formal setting. She looked into his ice blue eyes and realized his height matched hers even while she wore high heels.

"Good. We'll check it out."

She slid onto the passenger seat and he closed the door.

As his car merged with other vehicles speeding along the highway, Procne recalled not wanting to be alone with Roger in her home. Yet here she was now, alone with him in his car. What had she been thinking? In her home she knew neighbors were nearby. But who was nearby now? She glanced out the window and imagined leaping from the speeding vehicle. Not a good idea—her body would go "splat" on the pavement. If push came to shove, it would be better to use her high-heeled sandals as a weapon.

The car turned into a quiet lane shadowed by tall Douglas fir trees. She frowned as Roger eased it onto an overgrown, bumpy driveway. For a road leading to a classy restaurant it was in need of much repair. Roger guided the car up to a dilapidated yellow house and beside it came to a stop.

She shivered. "This doesn't look like much of a restaurant to me. For one thing, the building needs a new coat of paint."

"This isn't the restaurant. It's an old house that's on the market. I want to show you an artistic mural on the living room wall. It's unique, quite beautiful. Then we'll carry on to the restaurant."

They got out of the car and she carefully followed Roger up a few rickety steps. He unlocked the front door of the house and ushered her inside. She hesitated then walked slowly into the living room. Looking at the paint chipped walls, she shivered again.

No mural was in sight.

CHAPTER 40

Monday Evening

Philomela stood in front of the cook top and shifted chicken strips and vegetable chunks around the frying pan. The dish wasn't Chinese, East Indian, or Thai. It was strictly Philomela Stir-fry. It contained chicken, whatever vegetables were in the fridge, plus an array of spices. Each of her creations was slightly different from former ones. The best part of such a culinary dish was that only one cooking pan plus a pot for rice were needed. No other pots to scrub and clean.

Brent would have called it, "Another Philomela Special."

She had shopped for groceries before knowing Brent would not be here. So, after returning home from the museum and having lunch at the History Café, she had knocked on Mary Skidmore's front door and invited her to come over for dinner.

Philomela took two warmed plates from the oven and scooped rice and stir-fry onto them. In the dining room she set one plate in the place setting in front of Mary and one at the other place setting. She filled two glasses with water, set them beside two glasses of white wine, and sat down.

"Dig in while the Philomela Special is hot."

Mary swallowed a bite and nodded her head. "It's delicious."

"Oh, good. I'm never sure how it will turn out. If this hadn't been such a spur of the moment idea, I would have invited Procne for dinner, too. Oh well, I hope she's eating properly and not just nibbling on junk food."

"Junk food is fine once in a while," Mary said. "But I think Procne's too sensible to try and live on it."

"You're right. After moving here, I'll have to refrain from becoming a mother hen regarding her eating habits and other things. Procne would hate having me continually nag at her."

Mary chuckled and took another mouthful.

"Do you worry about living alone with a murderer on the loose?" Philomela asked.

"Occasionally. But I'm old and young women are the likely targets. Even so, I keep my doors locked and only let people in who I know and trust. I have a frying pan at the ready…to use as a weapon if necessary."

Procne chuckled. "Good idea."

When they finished eating, Mary suggested they go for a walk to help their food digest.

"Okay. Give me a jiffy to put the leftovers in the fridge."

A few minutes later, Philomela locked the door and dropped the key inside her purse. They walked in silence for almost a block, each occasionally glancing around as if expecting to see an undesirable person.

Mary was the first to speak. "Do you know if the police have any leads on finding the murderer?"

"I had lunch at the History Café today and Jean hadn't heard anything. She usually keeps abreast of everything happening in Saltaire. I haven't heard anything either."

"I hope they catch him soon. I'm old, but the idea of a demented kook wandering around often makes me feel squeamish. Murder is far worse than an ordinary home invasion. Back in my youth no one ever heard of a home invasion. And murder was something that occasionally happened elsewhere. Oh well, I must say it's a relief having you next door."

"I'll follow your advice and keep a heavy frying pan handy…in case a weapon is needed."

Mary chuckled.

The sun was low in the western sky and as they neared the ocean the air grew chillier. Philomela was glad she wore a light sweater. "Let's pop in on Procne."

"Do you think we should?"

"It's something I mustn't do when we live here permanently. But for now, it's probably okay."

They walked on the interlocking bricks up to the metal gate and peered into the open-air vestibule. Philomela pressed Procne's bell. No one answered. She pressed it again. After the third ring she said, "She's not at home."

"Probably a big date."

"Could be." Wondering if her sister was with Simon Fraser, Philomela turned away from the metal gate. She saw Selene walk toward them so waited until Procne's neighbor drew close. "Hi, Selene."

"Hello, Philomela and Mary. Are you looking for Procne?"

"Yes, we are."

"I saw her get into a gray car around six o'clock. She was wearing high-heel sandals and a pretty dress. Looked like a dinner date."

"Do you know who she was with?" Philomela recalled that Simon Fraser's SUV was dark blue.

"I didn't see the driver, so I don't know if it was a

man or a woman. But I have news about the murders. I saw Constable James this afternoon and she said they have a couple of leads."

"Good," Philomela said. "Do you know what kind of leads?"

"She implied that a new witness has come forward."

"That's encouraging."

"I don't know who the witness is, or how reliable he or she is. But at least things are moving forward."

Philomela nodded then asked, "How are you doing, Selene?"

"Excellent, thanks. Constable James asked—unofficially of course—if I could meditate on the murders. She hopes I'll give the police a few tips. I told her not to hold her breath. But I plan to meditate on it this evening."

"Good luck in zeroing in on the culprit."

As Mary and Philomela headed for home, Mary asked, "Do you think Selene really has psychic abilities?"

"I do. But her messages often appear unexpectedly and sometimes are quite vague. She readily admits when nothing comes to her."

"I've never visited her."

"She has a healing circle. As a nurse you might like to join them sometime."

"An old, out of date nurse."

"That doesn't matter.

They walked to Main Avenue and stopped in front of a coffee shop that sold ice cream. Looking at each other they burst out laughing. Then they went inside. Holding their cones and licking the ice cream they left the coffee shop and walked in companionable silence back home.

Alone in her house, Philomela phoned her sister. It was ten-fifteen and the answering machine came on. Philomela left no message.

She tried again at ten-fifty-five. The machine again came on.

Ready for bed, Philomela tried again at eleven-fifteen. This time she left a brief message: "Hi, sis. Hope you're having a lovely time. Phone me when you get home—no matter how late the hour."

Wondering where her sister was and who she was with, Philomela recalled Selene's words. She saw Procne around six p.m. and it was now eleven-fifteen. Five and a half hours was a long time to eat dinner.

Could she be spending the night at Simon Fraser's home? Possibly. Then again, it seemed unlikely because Selene said the car Procne got into was gray, not dark blue. Perhaps she should phone Simon.

Philomela gave herself a shake. Her kid sister was an adult. She had to let her do her own thing and live her own life.

CHAPTER 41

Tuesday Morning

Philomela listened to the phone ring. She knew Procne would be up before eight-thirty, so when the answering machine came on she felt a shiver of apprehension. Realizing her sister may be having a shower and unable to hear the phone, she relaxed.

Ten minutes later she phoned again. Again the machine's hollow voice answered. It crossed her mind that Simon Fraser may have bought a new car—a gray one—and she smiled wanly. Her apprehension returned as she wondered about Simon—he seemed a scholar and a gentleman who would never cheat on his wife, even under the dreadful current circumstances. But appearances often were deceiving. Could his friendship with Procne already have developed into something intimate? If so, with Angelina still alive, she suspected both Simon and Procne would suffer pangs of guilt.

No matter where her sister spent last night, Philomela was confident she would be at the dress shop in an hour. Or perhaps she was already there doing work before the shop opened to the public. She decided to check. She phoned Whimsical Woman. The answering machine answered.

Philomela's intake of breath faltered and her heartbeat speeded up. She told herself not to panic. Panic would solve nothing. She took a deep breath and exhaled loudly. Her heart beat faster and louder.

She needed to break her fast, so she boiled an egg, placed a slice of bread in the toaster, and gradually felt her heartbeat slow down. Her apprehension went in abeyance and she put the egg in a wooden egg cup. She set the food on the patio table in the dining area and began eating.

For no logical reason she recalled a conversation she and Brent had yesterday.

"Retirement will probably bore me," he had said.

"Unlikely," she had replied. "Several retired people have told me they wonder how they had time to work. They keep so busy volunteering, gardening, traveling, etc."

"Well, I could get interested in cars."

Philomela laughed. "You're already interested in them. You have the 1965 S-type Jaguar and it's bound to need lots of repairs."

"What about you? Will you be bored?"

"I'll be busy getting settled. Then I'll be busy learning about Northwest gardening...it will be different from gardening in the Rocky Mountain foothills. Occasionally I'll help Procne in the shop. If my curse of curiosity raises its ugly head I'll find a way to satisfy it. I might visit a local magazine office and offer to write articles for them. As a last resort I can always vacuum and dust. To answer your question—no, I won't be bored."

At nine-fifty, Philomela stopped ruminating. She locked up the house and walked briskly to Whimsical Woman. It took only ten minutes. The shop looked dark, the door was shut, and a sign inside its window said, *CLOSED*. Feeing extremely nervous, Philomela tried to open the door. It was locked. She knocked on the door and waited. No one responded. She banged on the door louder than before. Nobody appeared. The dress shop was as alive as a morgue.

Her apprehension disappeared—she was scared. Procne was committed to her shop. Only fire, flood, or death would keep her from opening it at its regular time. Shivers ran up and down Philomela's spine and she glanced at her watch. Ten-oh four a.m. Thirty-four minutes past opening time.

She scooted to the door of Upscale Garments. Opening it, she saw Sheila Trust, looking her usual classy self in smart black pants and a white angora sweater. She was counting out change for a customer. When the customer picked up her purchase and walked to the door, Philomela hurried to the cash counter and looked steadily at the owner.

"Sheila, have you talked with Procne recently?"

"Not since early yesterday afternoon. Why?"

"I can't find her. The shop hasn't been opened."

"What?" Sheila's eyebrows almost hit her front hairline. "That's not like Procne. She's dedicated to her shop."

"I know. I'll phone Selene Hamilton and see if she knows anything." Philomela took her cellphone from her purse and punched in the numbers. Holding the phone to her ear she greeted Procne's neighbor and explained her concern. After snapping the phone shut, she again gazed at Sheila. "Selene hasn't heard a peep. The last she saw of Procne was when she climbed into a gray car around six o'clock last evening. She said she'll knock on her door and call back."

"Should we phone the police?" Sheila asked.

"It's barely sixteen hours since Selene saw Procne get in the car, but because of recent events, I bet the police will consider her a missing person.

"So, are you going to phone them?"

"I'll wait until Selene calls back."

A few minutes later the call came. "I used my emergency key," Selene said.

"Procne isn't home. Her bed wasn't slept in."

"Thanks Selene. I'm going to visit the police station in person." Philomela pressed the off button.

Sheila nodded. "I'll keep an eye on her shop. Please keep me posted about what the police say."

"I will."

At the police station Philomela considered it lucky that Constable James was on duty. There was something to be said about knowing a policewoman who understood the problem. It also helped that the constable was sensible, practical, and had feminine sensitivities. After hearing Philomela's concern about her missing sister, the constable frowned and bit her lower lip. Then she said, "Because of the dire circumstances, I'll put Procne on the missing person's list right away."

"What can I do besides worry?" Philomela asked her.

"Keep your eyes and ears and nose open for subtle clues. If you get any idea where she might be, let me know."

Though everyone at the police station expressed concern and was kind and helpful, Philomela felt despondent. All she could think about was Kathy and Annette. They had disappeared one day and were found the next day—dead.

CHAPTER 42

Tuesday Morning, Continued.

P hilomela's thoughts whirled. Not wanting her sister to suffer Kathy's and Anette's fates, she mentally zeroed in on a mantra: "Procne is alive and well." Having said goodbye to the staff at the police station, she pounded the sidewalk and forlornly repeated the mantra, "Procne is alive and well."

Procne was such a super person, why would anyone want to kill her? That, of course, was what everyone said about the two young realtors—and neither of them had survived.

Unlike those two young women, Procne had the advantage of suspecting a serial killer might still be in town. Surely, she was too savvy to be caught alone by a manipulative murderer. Doubtless, she would be wary of anyone, man or woman, who seemed the least bit suspicious. But could she hold her own if unexpectedly attacked from behind? What could she do to protect herself if she was suddenly knocked on the head and rendered unconscious or injected with a high-powered opiate?

Not wanting to answer her own questions, Philomela phoned Sheila and told her that Procne was now considered a missing person. Continuing to walk toward her new home, she abruptly stopped in the middle of the sidewalk. A subtle clue clung to the edge of her mind. The clue was so nebulous that she figured the only person who might make sense of it was Selene. She made a one-hundred-and-eighty-degree turn then headed toward the townhouse complex her sister shared with six other people.

Philomela had been so distraught when talking with Constable James that the gray car Selene had mentioned slipped from her mind. Perhaps her brief memory loss would prove serendipitous. Selene would be more relaxed chatting with her than with the police, enhancing the chance of being able to visualize the gray car in more detail.

In reply to Philomela's question, Selene shook her head. "I don't know what make the car was. I'm not familiar with all their various shapes and logos."

They sat on one of Selene's soft blue and white loveseats and gazed at each other over the coffee table. Selene's round face and pale blue eyes reminded Philomela of the psychic's namesake—Selene, the mythical Greek moon goddess. Her long silvery-blue dress added to her airy moon goddess appearance. Surely all this, along with the peaceful ambience of Selene's sitting room, would help her shamanistic abilities to come into play. Surely, she would be able to visualize her missing neighbor getting into the gray car and with luck she might recognize the driver.

Philomela waited silently, optimistically hoping against hope that Selene would elaborate. The still air hung motionlessly between them and no one spoke. Finally, Philomela asked another question.

"Were you going out or coming in when you saw the car?"

"I was going out to meet a young girl suffering from severe post-partum depression. My plan was to give the young mother a break from all her responsibilities. Her husband cared for their baby and two year old son while I took her out for a quiet dinner. It gave us a chance to eat and talk without interruption. I stressed the need to pay attention to what she ate in case a food allergy was aggravating her depression."

Philomela nodded. Typical Selene. Always helping others.

"Getting briefly away from the responsibilities of house and children did raise her spirits, at least temporarily. If she can get more sleep that will help improve her optimism. I also suggested she take B vitamins—B-Three is often called the happy vitamin."

Philomela nodded again. She couldn't imagine having to feed a baby every three hours or so. Her thoughts shifted from the tired young mother to her own concerns. At the moment her sister was more important than a young woman's sleepless nights. She studied Selene and reiterated, "Last evening you were standing on the sidewalk when you saw Procne get in the gray car?"

"No, I was opening the metal gate of the open-air vestibule when I saw a man open the car door for her. She got in and he walked behind the car to the driver's side. I only saw his back. He was quite tall and seemed to have dark hair. As the metal gate shut behind me, I watched the car drive away."

"You didn't see his face?"

"No. From the back, he looked like dozens of other men."

"Did the gray car have four doors?"

"Mmm…Yes, it did."

"A sedan probably. Not a large SUV or a van?"

"It wasn't big, but not small either. It wasn't a convertible. But it was a pretty car."

"As it drove away, did you notice anything special on its rear end? Symbols? Prominent trunk? Anything at all?" Philomela hoped Selene's eidetic talent would come to the fore.

Selene closed her eyes and apparently saw the same image she had seen before. "Taillights. It has wide taillights. The trunk slopes down, inconspicuously. There is a symbol...a letter. I think it's a fancy capital L. It's above the license plate. There's printing on the left side of the license plate but it's too small to read."

"A fancy capital L? Do you know what the L indicates?" Philomela wished she had paid more attention to car manufacturers, their types of vehicles, and their logos. What she really needed was Brent. He could spot various car makes a block away.

Selene opened her eyes and shook her head. "I don't pay much attention to car styles."

"Me neither." Philomela's train of thought shifted from motorcars to Selene's innate gift of visualizing past happenings and future events. Then she wondered about the present. "Do you have a fervid feeling about Procne's whereabouts at this precise moment?" She really wanted to ask if the psychic thought her sister was dead, but she was unable to formulate the words.

"I don't think she's dead, if that's what you're implying."

Philomela nodded with relief. As always, the psychic surprised her by tapping into her exact thought. Whether or not she truly believed in Selene's psychic powers, she figured that mental telepathy often came into play. "Do you know where Procne is right now?" she asked.

"In a dark room."

Philomela felt every nerve of her body go on alert. "Where is this dark room?"

"I don't know. I can't get a clear picture. It's too dark. She's lying down. She seems to be struggling." Selene closed her eyes again. Then she opened them and shook her head. "I'm sorry, Philomela, that's the best I can do. At least for now. Maybe something clearer will come later on."

"That's a start, Selene. At least you think she's still alive. I'll phone the police and suggest they start looking for a gray car with the letter L above the license plate. No, first I'll contact Brent and ask him what the fancy L stands for."

She phoned Brent. He was outside at the well site, and he promptly answered her call. She politely asked how he and the well were doing, and he replied that the well problems were now solved and he was anxious to get back to Saltaire. Refraining from telling him that Procne was missing, she said that she and Selene wondered about car logos. Without hesitation Brent answered her question regarding the mysterious "L."

"Lexus."

"Lexus," she repeated. "I should have thought of that. Thanks, Brent. You're a life-saver. I'll be glad when you get back here." After saying goodbye, she shut off her cellphone and pulled Constable James's card from her purse.

Before Philomela could punch in any numbers, Selene said, "If you mention the dark room, you realize the police will ask how you learned about it. If you tell them I envisioned it, they'll hem and haw and laugh. Psychics are not their favorite witnesses. They think we're nuts."

Philomela couldn't help but laugh. "Police aren't the only ones who refuse to believe in telepathy and clairvoyance. Most people think visions and intuition are unreal, products of an over-active imagination. They believe that folks who experience such mental feats are illogical and peculiar, but not necessarily nuts."

Now it was Selene's turn to laugh. "I've been called illogical, peculiar, and nuts before. I've even been called a charlatan." Her humor faded as she leaned back and again shut her eyes. Hecate, her black cat, suddenly jumped up on her lap and started to purr. Selene opened her eyes and her fingers automatically stroked the cat's back. "Nothing is coming up."

Philomela watched her for a few minutes, willing the psychic to be more specific about Procne's whereabouts. Finally, she gave up and broke the silence. "Selene, as far as I know, the police have no leads and no clues. I'll tell them about the gray Lexus then casually mention the dark room. They may not take the latter seriously, but at least it will be planted in their subconscious for future use." She punched in the numbers of Constable James's cellphone.

CHAPTER 43

Tuesday Afternoon

Philomela walked from Selene's townhouse and thought how wonderful it would be if Olympus housed a real live goddess—a goddess who could discern the present and foresee the future. Though she lived in Olympus, she was not a goddess and would likely never develop those mysterious gifts.

However, she was confident her meeting with Selene had been worthwhile. Three important things had been more or less confirmed. First, Procne was alive. Second, the car she had entered last evening was a gray Lexus—she mentally thanked Brent for enlightening her about the capital "L." Third, the place Procne was in right now was very dark. Its identity and location remained a mystery. Was she in the basement of a house, in a closet, in a boarded-up barn, or in the trunk of a car? And Selene had said she was lying down.

Before leaving the psychic's townhouse, Philomela had been uplifted by Constable James's appreciative response to her phone call. "We'll check gray Lexus vehicles immediately," she had said. Her interest in the dark room was less apparent, but to her credit she didn't discount it completely.

Philomela thought of how lifestyles today revolved around information and transportation. Information arrived by cellphones, iPads, computers, old-fashioned telephones, and snail mail. Transportation was made in airplanes, trains, cars, trucks, vans, and SUVs. Back in her youth, cars were a luxury, so most people used shanks ponies—in other words they walked a great deal. Today, every university and high school student seemed to have a vehicle—bicycle, motor bike, skateboard, or car. Even in a town like Saltaire, where walking was easy and restaurants and shops were close by, cars filled the streets. The drivers were of female and male persuasions and from ages sixteen to ninety-seven.

Philomela wondered if the murderer was still in the area. Convinced that the perpetrator was a man, she tried to recall the types of cars driven by the men she had met a year and a half ago. The only reason she knew their car choices was because cars had helped solve Maxine Springer's murder. Of course, since then they could have sold their cars and bought new ones.

She remembered that Melvin Springer drove a black Range Rover, Simon Fraser drove a dark blue SUV, and Tom Trust drove a green Cadillac. At the moment she couldn't think of anyone else. Oh, yes, Grace Devonshire's vehicle had been British Racing Green. Today Tom Trust drove a new white Cadillac. And Brent was now the proud owner of an old racing-green S-type Jaguar.

The dark room was a worry. Even more worrisome was Selene's remark about Procne lying down and struggling. Why was Procne struggling? Was she bound and gagged? Was she struggling against her captor? Or was she mentally struggling with herself for having made a bad decision to get inside the gray car.

Philomela herself felt helpless and useless.

However, feeling sorry about her own plight was self-indulgent, a waste of time, of no help to her sister. She closed her eyes and tried to think objectively. The police would be looking for a gray Lexus. She could do the same.

At home, she used the phonebook and computer to obtain the addresses of some of the men she knew. Then she drove Brent's red truck to Main Avenue and parked near the museum. Basil Devonshire, Hamish MacDonald, and Simon Fraser might be there. She got out of the truck and studied every car on the street and in nearby parking lots. Not one gray car contained a fancy L above the back license plate.

She returned to the truck and drove to two grocery stores. She wandered up and down the parking lots studying the rear of every gray car. She knew full well she resembled a poor soul with memory problems who could not recall where she had parked her car. Shades of Alzheimer's.

In the parking lot of a third grocery store, excitement filled her body. She gazed at a gray vehicle with a fancy "L" above the license plate. Almost immediately a lady with a cartload of groceries walked over to it, opened the trunk, and proceeded to put grocery bags in it. Philomela sauntered near her and stopped.

"That's a beautiful car," she said.

"Thank you. I like driving it."

"Have you had it long?"

"Almost a year."

"Do you share it with your husband or partner?"

"No, this two-door car is mine. My husband has a Lexus, too. His has four doors."

"I don't suppose he would be interested in selling it."

She chuckled. "No. He likes it too well. Our cars are matched sets...both gray."

"I'm Philomela Nightingale." She held out her hand and hoped the woman didn't notice it twitch with excitement.

The woman shook it. "I'm Sharon Webb."

"It's been nice talking with you, Sharon. Enjoy your car."

Philomela smiled at her, walked toward Brent's truck, and surreptitiously watched the woman close the trunk of her car. As the woman pushed the empty grocery cart to the covered lineup of other empty carts, Philomela jotted down the woman's name and license plate number in her little book.

Next she drove past Basil Devonshire's home and had bad luck. No car sat in his driveway or out in front on the street. She had similar bad luck at the condominium where Hamish MacDonald lived and at the house belonging to Melvin Springer. Though confident Simon Fraser had no vehicle with a fancy L, she drove past his house anyway. No such vehicle was in sight.

She concluded that if it wasn't for bad luck she'd have no luck at all.

Feeling less than optimistic, she drove near the office of Trust Realty. She parked the truck and then on foot checked the gray cars on both sides of the street. None sported a fancy L. She walked to the parking area behind the office building and spotted a gray, four-door sedan parked between a white Cadillac and a red Honda. Feeling excited, she hurried toward it and almost bumped into two men walking toward her. In animated conversation, they stopped behind the gray car, apparently oblivious of her desire to see the license plate.

She caught a glimpse of the fancy L above the license plate, but as the two men's voices grew louder, she wandered from the parking lot to the nearby corner. It was a four-way-stop for vehicles with a prominent pedestrian crosswalk. She walked across the street to a coffee shop, went inside, bought a small coffee, then carried it outside and sat down at an empty table. She stared across the street at the entrance to the parking lot. Sipping her coffee, she watched motor vehicles drive past her, stop at the pedestrian crosswalk, and then proceed forward.

The day was warm and watching people and vehicles was a pleasant pastime. Even so, she could only make her coffee last so long. Finally, she went inside, bought a second cup of coffee, and returned outside to reclaim her same table with the clear view of the entrance to the parking lot. Glancing at her watch and wondering if Brent was now flying over Saskatchewan, she peripherally saw the white Cadillac come out of the parking lot. It turned in the direction away from the four-way stop. She recognized the driver—Tom Trust. Doubtless the man beside him was a client, a prospective buyer.

She sipped her coffee and wondered about his appearance the other night at her door. Was he really just checking to make sure she was okay?

A large double-decker bus came and stopped right beside her. She gazed into the faces of passengers in both upper and lower decks. Apparently, foot traffic on the crosswalk was heavy because two cars in front of the bus waited a few minutes. When all three vehicles finally moved forward, she peered at the parking lot across the street. A gray car was turning in the same direction as the white Cadillac. She saw the rear end of the car but couldn't read the license plate number and wasn't sure if she saw a big "L." Nor could she see who was driving it.

She suspected it was the Lexus that had been in the parking lot.

She regretted allowing the two loud men to intimidate her. They had prevented her from jotting down the all-important license plate numbers.

The white Cadillac belonged to Tom Trust. Could the gray car belong to Roger Thistle or to Myrtle, the one remaining female realtor at Trust Realty? If memory served her correctly, Roger's car had been gray or blue. While following him to view houses, she had not noticed any symbol or printing—so his car could be a Toyota, Honda, Chevrolet, Ford, or any of the other dozens of cars on the road systems. And to think she had actually been inside the car. Annoyed with her failure to notice such details, she shook her head. What was happing to her excellent powers of observation?

Cataracts? Alzheimer's? She hoped neither.

What should she do now? Though her information was incomplete, there seemed only one thing to do.

She drained her coffee cup, carried the empty mug inside the coffee shop and left it on the countertop. Outside again, she took her cellphone from her purse, called Constable James, and received voice mail. She left a message, giving the license plate number for Sharon Webb's two-door Lexus and explained that her husband had a four-door gray Lexus. Philomela also explained seeing a gray Lexus sitting in the Trust Realty parking lot and apologized for not obtaining the license number. She suggested the constable should check out Webb's four-door gray sedan and Roger Thistle's car.

She made her way back to Brent's truck and climbed inside. Like a bird perched on a high tree branch, she studied the world around her. She hadn't done much, but at least she had given the police another tip.

But where in the world was Procne?

CHAPTER 44

Tuesday Afternoon, Later

Philomela entered her house and listened. Hearing nothing amiss, she looked around and bravely marched to the kitchen. She dropped her purse on the counter, hurriedly opened the pot and pan drawer, and took out the new frying pan. Holding it at the ready in her right hand, she walked through the dining and living rooms, tip-toed down the hall and checked the en-suite master bedroom and the smaller bedroom and bathroom. She was alone—on the main floor.

She switched on the light and walked nervously downstairs to the basement. Again nothing was amiss. She checked the windows and felt confident no one could get inside—unless they smashed the glass.

Back on the main floor, she sat down on a patio chair in the dining room and considered the time of day. It wasn't dark outside, but that didn't matter. The murderer had apparently latched onto his first two victims during daylight hours.

Why was she becoming such a worrier? No murderer would bother killing her. She was past middle age, and she was not a full-time resident of Saltaire. Nor was she a realtor.

But would he go after her sister? Except for being young, good looking, and female, Procne had little else in common with Kathy and Annette. Unlike the two victims, she was not a realtor. She moved in different work circles and traveled in different social whirls.

But all three knew many of the same people. All three enjoyed their jobs and were good at them. Doubtless they shared a few personality traits—pleasant, capable, self-confident, and successful. Would those traits be reason enough for someone to murder them?

Surely not.

Philomela wracked her brain for another reason. Perhaps Annette and Kathy were sexual teasers who led the murderer on and then dumped him at a critical moment. Or perhaps they owed him money. Money caused a lot of problems. Philomela had not heard of any debt problems, but she had been in contact with both victims for only a short period of time. As far as she knew, Procne owed no one any money except for the mortgage on her townhouse.

A muted ringing interrupted her rumination. She ran to the kitchen, grabbed her purse, and took out her cellphone. Hoping it was Procne on the other end of the line, she said, "Hello."

"Philomela, Constable James here. I'm phoning to thank you for the leads on the gray Lexus. Mr. and Mrs. Webb have airtight alibis. They just returned two days ago from a holiday in Europe."

"Okay."

"We're checking for the owner of the gray Lexus near the office of Trust Realty. I'll let you know the results. Have you heard anything from Procne?"

"Nothing."

"Keep in touch with me. If you think of anything, please give me a call."

"I will."

Philomela returned to the dining room and slumped onto a patio chair. She glanced around at the temporary furniture and her rumination resurfaced. She recollected the morning of Kathy Holmes's no-show. Feeling agitated, she and Brent had returned to the Seaside Motel. He had phoned Trust Realty to complain and that was when she had first heard the names of Annette Murphy and Roger Thistle.

For the second time, her rumination was interrupted by the ringing of her cellphone. She hurried back to the kitchen, hit the talk button, and said "Hello."

"Constable James here, Philomela. I want you to know that a four-door gray Lexus is owned by Roger Arthur Thistle. We're trying to locate him to ask if he had any contact with Procne last evening. So far, we haven't succeeded in reaching him. He doesn't answer his phone and he isn't at home or at the office. Apparently he's showing houses to a client."

Philomela thanked the constable for giving her the new information then pressed the off button. She thought about Roger Arthur Thistle.

The first initials of his name spelled rat. Did the acronym have a hidden meaning? Good grief, she was really grasping for straws. After all, what's in a name? A rose by any other name would smell the same. She agreed with Shakespeare on that matter—a name didn't make the person.

She resumed her rumination. When Brent had phoned to complain about Kathy's no-show, Annette answered and then gave the phone to Roger. A couple of days later, Annette mentioned that Roger had assured her that Brent and Philomela were his clients.

At the time, she had paid little attention to Annette's remark because it seemed unimportant. Now she wondered if Roger had purposely misinformed Annette in order to obtain a new client. It was a strange thing for him to do, especially when Kathy could have reappeared at any moment to reclaim them as her clients.

Then she had a chilling thought—had Roger known Kathy would never again physically appear?

Philomela's first impulse was to phone the constable. Before punching in the numbers, she realized her idea was based only on speculation. She had only innuendo and suspicion. No hard facts, no real clues. Just woman's intuition.

If Roger was the guilty party, where would he have taken Procne? The dark room Selene envisioned could be anywhere. However, it would have to be where no one would casually find her. The most logical place would be the basement of his house, provided he lived by himself or else with a co-kidnapper/murderer.

Having no idea about Roger's personal life, she decided to phone Tom Trust and ask him. Then she thought better of it because Tom might casually mention her call and thereby alert Roger. Both men were on her murder suspect list. The last thing she wanted to do was make either Tom or Roger aware of her suspicions.

She picked up the phone book and flipped to the Ts. She found the black printed address and phone number of Trust Realty. She then found Roger Thistle's name but no address was given.

In desperation, she called Selene and asked if she'd had any more thoughts about Procne.

"Nothing, Philomela. I've received not a twinge of her health or of her whereabouts. Maybe it's because we're good friends and as a result I'm too close to her."

Philomela blurted out, "Roger Thistle drives a four-door gray Lexus." She hoped this might trigger some sort of response in Selene's psyche.

"How do you know?"

"After seeing a gray Lexus in Trust Realty's parking lot, I contacted Constable James. She checked it out then phoned back and told me."

"Mmm. Do you know where Roger lives?"

"No. He's listed in the phone book but no address is given."

"Do you think Roger could be the guilty party?"

"Selene, I honestly don't know."

"Until we know for sure, there's not much we can do."

"Looks like a dead end, Selene."

"I'm afraid so."

"Thanks. Keep in touch."

Philomela shut off her cellphone and glanced briefly out the window. Then she checked the phone numbers for Upscale Garments. Sheila answered her call on the second ring. On the pretext of wanting to ask Roger a question about interior design, Philomela asked Sheila if he lived in a house.

"He's renting an apartment, Philomela. A month or so ago he talked with Tom about buying a condominium. So far, it hasn't happened."

"Thanks, Sheila. Procne told me he had helped a few people with design problems. I might just wander over to your husband's office and speak with him."

"There's no doubt he has a flare for design. He gave me good advice for a window problem. But I didn't take it—nice but too artsy-fartsy for me. I'm sure he'd be happy to try and help you."

After shutting off her phone, Philomela leaned back in her patio chair and closed her eyes. In the depths of her mind, she imagined every man she could think of as a murderer. She eliminated everyone...except Roger Arthur Thistle. Where could Roger have taken Procne?

She refused to believe that her sister might already be dead.

CHAPTER 45

Tuesday Afternoon, Much Later

L ooking out the window at the bright western sky, Philomela thought how ironical that on this warm and beautiful autumn afternoon she was sitting in her new home with windows and doors closed and locked. She was behaving like a prisoner. Why? Because of fear—fear of the unknown. Fear of a murderer.

Who was the murderer?

Where was he?

Where was her kid sister?

She had no idea why Procne was missing. It was uncharacteristic of her to disappear without a trace. She had too much empathy to leave her friends and relatives in a frenzy of worry. Did that mean she had been unwillingly taken away?

What else could explain her absence?

Knowing that sitting here like a Zombie would not bring her sister back home, she wondered what else she could do. Like a dedicated nun, could she pray to God for help? Like Buddha, could she sit in a lotus position and meditate? Or like a faithful member of the Islamic religion, could she bend on all fours facing Mecca? Or like a glutton, could she revive herself with food?

Philomela glanced at her wristwatch. Five-thirty p.m. She wasn't a real glutton, but a bite to eat and a brief chat with Jean Greenfield at the History Café seemed like a good idea. Jean was so logical and so down to earth—she might have an idea about where to search for Procne.

Philomela dropped her cellphone in her purse and stood up. Murderer be damned, she could easily walk to the History Café. Then again, she could also drive Brent's truck. With most shops closed there would be ample parking on Main Avenue.

She parked the red truck close to the History Café and went inside. Jean was bustling behind the counter. Except for three men sitting at a table in a corner, the place was free of customers—too late for afternoon tea and a too early for dinner. Jean looked over at the new arrival and smiled.

"Hello, Philomela. How are you?"

"I'm fine, Jean. But Procne still hasn't turned up."

Jean frowned and slowly shook her head. Then she murmured, "That's so unlike her."

"I know. The police are looking for her and Selene is trying to envision her. I'm doing my best to keep my wits about me. I simply don't know what to do. Do you have any suggestions?"

"Do you think the murderer has her?"

"That's my biggest fear. Selene saw her yesterday at six o'clock—almost twenty-four hours ago...get into a four-door gray Lexus."

"Who was driving the Lexus?"

"Selene saw the back of the driver, but couldn't identify him. She said he has dark hair. No one else has come up with any information. The police are searching for the owners of gray Lexus cars."

"Philomela, here's my suggestion. You need nourishment to keep your energy from flagging."

"I was just going to have coffee."

"You need real food. Fish chowder with French bread. Coffee on the side."

A few minutes later, Jean walked around the counter and set chowder, bread, oil and vinegar on a table. "Sit down and eat the chowder. I'll get some coffee for you. It's on the house."

"Oh, no, Jean. You're too generous"

"Not at all. Eat."

Philomela obeyed her. Taking a sip of chowder she realized Jean was right—she really did need nourishment. Knowing it raised her low blood sugar level, she appreciatively swallowed a few more spoonfuls. Jean reappeared with two mugs of coffee and set one in front of Philomela. Holding the other in her left hand she sat down across the table from her worried customer.

"What does your husband think of Procne's disappearance?"

"He doesn't know about it. He was called back to work in Saskatchewan. He's a good problem solver. I contacted him about the Logo on the gray car but didn't worry him about Procne."

Jean sighed. "We need a good problem solver here."

"That's true. I'm counting on the police."

Jean quietly sipped her coffee then set the mug on the table and studied Philomela. "Let's hope Procne's off on a romantic tryst with a handsome Prince Charming."

"I wish. But, Jean, you and I know she wouldn't worry us like this. Somehow she'd let us know she was fine. If the so-called Prince Charming is a killer, we have to think like he does." Philomela gazed pensively at the café owner and murmured, "That's easier said than done. My first question is—why would he want to hurt Procne? She not a realtor."

"No, but she's young and female. And like Kathy and Annette, she's good looking and successful."

Philomela nodded. "Maybe the perpetrator hates women."

"Or perhaps he hates women of a specific age. Annette and Kathy were in their most productive years. As is Procne." Jean took another sip of coffee.

"Or does he hate honest, successful women?" Philomela closed her eyes. "The two victims and Procne were successful."

"Or does he just kill randomly?" Jean asked.

"We know the two who were killed…where they were killed…and how they were killed. Kathy was killed in a vacant house in the early evening. Annette was killed in a house one afternoon while the owners were away for a couple of days. The killer obviously knew when the houses would be empty."

Jean's eyebrows raised in surprise. "Do you think the killer is a realtor?"

"Possibly. But non-realtors could easily get that information by making a phone call or two. Selene thinks Procne is in a dark room, maybe a car trunk or a basement." Philomela gazed at her dark brew and a few tacky houses came to mind. She recalled one in particular that was a real wreck. Roger had explained that the land had possibilities for someone who wanted to build, but the shack was a tear-down. They hadn't even bothered to go inside the tumble-down shack. She and Brent had not been the least bit interested in it.

Now it interested her. Her stomach muscles tightened and her interest in the shack increased.

She paid for her chowder and thanked Jean for the free coffee. "Talking with you about the murders makes me feel confident Procne is still alive. You're a good friend, Jean. You and the chowder were what I needed to perk me up. I owe you big time."

"Not at all," Jean said.

Four dinner customers came inside and Philomela hurried to the door of the café. Without a backward glance she went outside.

CHAPTER 46

Tuesday Evening

In Brent's truck, she headed for the dilapidated house. She couldn't remember the address, but she had a good idea where it was located. After a few wrong turns, she spotted the twisty overgrown lane and turned into it. She drove up to the shack with the peeling yellow paint and the two windows covered with plywood. Not wanting to advertise her presence there, she drove her truck around to the back of the tumble-down house and parked.

She climbed out of the truck and walked to the back door. It was locked. She walked to the front door. It also was locked. She went around to the back again and jiggled the door back and forth. Pulling it in and out, she felt something give way and heard a loud snap.

To her surprise she was able to push the door open. She really hadn't expected to get inside the house so easily.

She walked inside and her breathing was almost overcome with dusty and musty smells. She stepped into a kitchen whose floor was littered with junk that covered other junk. Dust was everywhere. Stopping near a cracked sink, she listened and heard only silence. She tip-toed through a living/dining area then went into what was once a bedroom. She returned to the kitchen, opened a door, and peered down a staircase into dank darkness. She heard a scurrying sound. Rats, she thought.

Should she venture down the stairs? The thought made her shiver. Noticing a light switch on the wall near her shoulder, she flicked it. Nothing happened. Obviously there was no electricity.

With the setting sun streaming through a window be-hind her, she walked down three steps. She carefully made her way down three more steps and paused, hoping her eyes would adjust to the darkness. They did, allowing her to see the floor of the basement. She gingerly made her way to the bottom of the stairs and realized the floor was not concrete. It was dirt.

She heard a different sound, one that reminded her of a cat's meow. Was that the sound that rats made? She didn't know. Thinking an animal might be in distress she took four steps toward the sound and stopped.

"Anybody here?" She spoke softly, not wanting to startle the unknown animal.

She was rewarded with the same meowing sound.

Stepping carefully along the dirt floor she moved to-ward the sound. "Hello," she said.

The meowing sound came again.

She smelled something that reminded her of urine. Her shin hit something hard and refraining from cursing she muttered a soft "Ouch." She bent down and her hands felt some sort of metal frame. She reached beyond the frame and her fingers grasped fabric that felt like scratchy wool. The dim light flowing down the stairway and through a nearby filthy window helped her eyes see the outline of an old metal bedstead. A blanket lay on top of the springs. The blanket moved.

Startled, Philomela gasped and jumped backward. She squinted at the blanket. Was a cat or perhaps a rat under it?

The meowing sound came again. "Mmm, mmm, mmm." It sounded less like a cat and more like a human being,

Philomela's heartbeat increased. Her right hand trembled as it crawled along the blanket to what felt like the curve of a shoulder, a neck, and a face. Could it be her sister? Feeling duct tape, she exclaimed, "Good grief. Your mouth is taped shut."

The only answer was another "Mm mmm."

Her fingers grasped a corner of the duct tape and she gently tried to pry the tape away from the mouth. It obviously caused the person discomfort. Finally, in desperation, Philomela simply yanked the tape off the face.

"Ooh, ouch."

"Sorry."

"Philomela?" The voice was weak.

"Procne? Is that you?"

"Yes."

Relief flooded Philomela's entire being. "Are you okay?"

"I don't know. Thank goodness you're here." Procne's shoulders rose and fell as she started to sob. "Until a minute ago I thought I was a goner."

"Who did this to you?" Philomela's body tensed in anger. She felt akin to their Greek myth namesakes who had committed a murder. Like the mythical Procne and Philomela, right now she felt capable of killing her sister's kidnapper and potential killer.

Between sobs Procne managed to answer her sister's question. "Roger...Roger Thistle."

"So, Roger's the guilty party. I didn't suspect him until about an hour ago."

Procne's sobs lessened. "My hands are in front of me. They're tied. My feet are tied to the bedstead. Can you undo them?"

Philomela's fingers found a cord circling Procne's wrists. The knot was double, but with a little twisting she managed to untie it.

"That's better." Procne rubbed each wrist with the opposite hand.

Philomela's fingers pulled back the rough blanket and found another cord circling Procne's ankles. Her fingers followed it to the short metal post at the left side of the foot of the bed. It took considerable effort, but she finally managed to untie the knots.

With ankles freed, Procne sighed. "I can barely move my feet or bend my knees."

"Are you able to sit up?" Philomela asked.

"I hope so. I'm awfully stiff and sore."

Philomela put her hands under Procne's arm pits and helped ease her body to a sitting position. Then she helped her sister swing her legs over the side of the jagged bed springs. "Not a very comfortable place to rest."

"You're not kidding. Philomela, when you came down the stairs I was so scared. I thought you were Roger. He told me he intends to choke me with a sky-blue silk tie."

"Sky-blue? Is there any significance to that?"

"Yes. The blue apparently matches the color of my eyes. Kathy's tie was brown to match her eyes. Annette's was turquoise to match hers."

"How do you know all this?"

"He told me."

"Is he coming back?"

"Yeah. Anytime soon."

"We have to get out of here. Are your legs able to walk up the stairs?"

"I'll try."

"We've got to leave before Roger returns. He may already suspect the police are searching for him."

Philomela half carried her sister to the stairs. Then she helped Procne put an arm around her shoulders and they slowly made their way up the steps. Halfway up, Procne lost her balance and Philomela tried desperately to keep both of them from tumbling backward. It was touch and go, but they regained their balance and continued moving upward. They made it to the main level. In the kitchen Procne leaned against a wall and took several deep breaths. Philomela was concerned about her sister's stiff muscles as well as her lack of energy. She probably hadn't eaten since lunch yesterday.

"Why do the police suspect Roger?" Procne asked.

"Selene told me she saw you get into a gray car about six o'clock. She remembered a big L on the back of the car. Brent said the vehicle was probably a Lexus. I contacted Constable James and she checked the owners of such cars. One of the owners was Roger Thistle." She took Procne's right arm. "Come on. Let's walk toward the back door. Brent's truck is parked behind the house."

They stumbled to the truck and after helping Procne laboriously climb into the passenger seat, Philomela walked around the back of the vehicle to the driver's side. Opening the door, she thought she heard the sound of an approaching car. Was it driving up the overgrown driveway? Yes, without question. The motor stopped and a car door slammed shut.

"Good grief! He's here." She listened and thought she heard a door squeak open. Doubtless Roger had a key to the front door of the shack. She hurriedly climbed into the truck and waited several seconds, giving him time to go inside and downstairs. She thought she saw a light in the kitchen near the basement door

"Did he have a flashlight?' she asked Procne.

"Yeah, he did."

As the light faded, she started the engine, backed up, and drove the truck along the side of the paint peeling shack. There on the middle of the narrow road was a gray Lexus. She would have to scrape some bushes to get past it. She saw no sign of Roger.

She eased the truck forward toward the Lexus. Peripherally she glimpsed Roger come out the front door to the top step. As he dashed down the rickety steps, she pressed the pedal to the metal. He ran toward them. The right side of the truck missed the Lexus by inches, and the left side scraped leaves and thorns of blackberry bushes. Not worrying about the truck's paint job, she whizzed along the twisty driveway to the road and then drove madly into town. Instead of going home or to the police department, she headed toward the hospital. She saw the Lexus follow them. As she turned into the emergency area of the hospital, the gray car was hot on the truck's tail.

"You need to be seen by a doctor," Philomela said, trying to sound relaxed though her heart beat like the drum of a military tattoo.

"I'm okay," Procne insisted. "He didn't rape me."

"Thank God for that. But you've had little food and you've been tied in an uncomfortable position for a long time. I'll bet you're dehydrated, too."

"I am thirsty."

Philomela parked in front of the emergency entrance. She opened the truck door and jumped out. She ran to the hospital, yanked open the door, and screamed, "Help. I need help."

She looked behind her and stared into Roger glaring eyes.

CHAPTER 47

Tuesday Evening, Much Later

A nurse ran outside the emergency door, and Roger threw his arms around Philomela. "It's okay. I can look after my wife."

"No," Philomela screamed. "He's not my husband. Don't let him touch my sister. He wants to kill her. She's in the truck. She needs our help."

Philomela struggled and Roger held her tightly. She kicked him in the shins. He loosened his grip on her, and she pulled free from him. She dashed back to the truck and opened the passenger door.

She helped her bedraggled sister slide out from the truck and guided her toward the hospital door. She saw the nurse glance with indecision at Roger then stare at Procne. Obviously noting Procne's stained attire and weakened physical state, the nurse ran over and helped Philomela. Together they slowly moved Procne through the doorway, past the triage area, and into the inner sanctum. The nurse guided them to a cubicle. She helped Procne remove her stained clothing, slip into a white hospital gown, and climb into bed. She closed curtains around the bed and adjusted some machinery. A few minutes later, a receptionist came in and obtained information from both sisters.

Philomela, worried about Roger's whereabouts, left the inner sanctum and walked through the waiting area to the outside door. She opened it and gazed outside. There was no sign of Roger or his gray Lexus. She hoped he had driven far away.

She returned to her sister's cubicle. "You okay, Procne?"

"I'm fine. All this fuss isn't necessary."

"Of course it is."

At that moment, a doctor entered and asked Procne a few general questions. He took her blood pressure, checked the pupils in each eye, and placed his stethoscope over her heart and lungs. He agreed she was dehydrated, but not badly enough to warrant an intravenous feeding of glucose and water. He said a glass of water and some food would make her feel better. He poured water into a glass that was sitting on the bedside table, helped her sit up, and handed the water to her. She swallowed half of it in what seemed two gulps.

The doctor left and a woman who could have been a nurse, a lab technician, or a cleaning lady entered the cubicle and placed a tray on the bedside table. She applied a tourniquet to Procne's upper arm, injected a needle into a vein, and pulled blood into the syringe.

Next, a person came with a bowl of soup, some crackers, and a bunch of grapes.

Procne thanked the food deliverer and sat up on the bed. She picked up the soup spoon and swallowed a mouthful of soup. "Tastes good."

Philomela, knowing her sister had been deprived of food and drink for a day and a half, watched her gobble up every morsel then drink a bit more water.

The nurse returned and Procne said, "I could run a marathon. I'm so happy to be alive. That was the best soup I've ever tasted."

The nurse chuckled. "That's a switch. Most patients can't say enough bad things about hospital food."

Philomela again walked out to the waiting room and stepped outside. She looked around the parking lot and seeing no sign of Roger Thistle, she phoned Constable James. "Roger Thistle kidnapped Procne," she said. "He tied her up in the basement of an old, abandoned house and left her in a cramped position on a filthy bed all last night and all day today. We're at emergency right now. She's okay and I don't think they'll keep her here overnight."

The constable spoke in an ominous tone of voice. "We still haven't been able to track down Roger Thistle. Do you know where he is?"

"His Lexus was behind us in the hospital emergency parking area. But he's gone now."

"Philomela, stay near Procne. Roger might try and cause her serious damage. He knows she could testify against him for kidnapping."

Philomela swallowed a large lump in her throat. Constable James meant more than serious damage, she meant fatal damage.

"We'll send someone to the hospital immediately," the constable said. "In the meantime, Procne must not be left alone."

"I'll stay with her." It flitted across Philomela's mind that she, too, could testify against Roger.

"We'll continue searching for Roger. What kind of vehicle are you driving?"

"Brent's red Chevrolet truck."

After shutting off her cellphone, Philomela walked back inside the emergency area and stopped at the nurse's desk. The nurse looked up. "Your sister is fine," she announced. "The food is raising her blood sugar and she'll soon be able to leave."

Philomela returned to Procne's cubicle and, five minutes later, Constable James walked in. She asked the victim a few questions then told Philomela she was going to join the search for Roger. "We've notified the airport and the ferry terminals, so his chance of getting off the island is nil. But the sooner we catch him, the better. A policeman will frequently check on you two."

Half an hour later, Philomela drove Procne away from the emergency parking lot. En route to Procne's town-home, she kept glancing in the rearview mirror for any sign of a gray Lexus. None appeared. Parking on the street outside the five-unit complex, she knew Roger would recognize Brent's vehicle and conclude they were in Procne's townhouse. She told Procne about her concern.

With purpose, they walked to the metal gate of the open-air vestibule. Standing outside it, Philomela pressed Selene's buzzer. When the psychic answered, Philomela asked if they could come in. The gate unlocked and Philomela pulled it open. They entered the vestibule and waited for Selene to open her door.

She did, and her shock at seeing her neighbor's disheveled appearance was apparent. She gasped loudly and stared at her neighbor. "Oh my goodness, Procne. Are you okay?"

As if on guard duty, Hecate, with black tail twitching, stood beside Selene's black pant leg. Philomela briefly feared he might screech and fly up and scratch his two uninvited visitors. But he didn't.

Philomela raised her eyes from the cat to Selene's pale blue eyes and was reminded of two silver dollars. She glanced at the psychic's dove-like silvery-gray top and crow-like black pants, but the glance was fleeting. Admiring sartorial splendor was the last thing on any of their minds.

"Selene," Philomela said. "May we come in?"

"Of course." Flustered, Selene stared at Procne's pale face and opened the door wide.

"I know I'm a sight," Procne said. "But you should have seen me before I got cleaned up at the hospital," Procne grinned at her neighbor. "I feel almost presentable now."

The two unexpected visitors walked inside and, without a word, Selene closed and locked the door. She led them to her sitting area and Hecate followed them. His tail gradually ceased twitching.

Procne hesitated to sit on a blue and white loveseat.

"Sid down, Procne," Selene said. "You won't hurt the fabric. It's washable."

As the sisters sat down, Selene politely asked, "Would you like something to eat or drink?"

"I'd love a glass of wine," Procne said.

"Me, too." Philomela grinned at her hostess. "I think we've earned one."

The room of soothing blues and whites seemed to help all three relax. Holding a stemmed glass of wine in her right hand, Procne related the saga of her kidnapping to both her sister and her friend. No one else said a word until she finished.

"You," Selene murmured, "are lucky to be alive."

Procne nodded her head. "I know."

"Do the police have Roger in custody?"

"I don't know," Philomela said. "They hadn't located him when we left the hospital." Suddenly, tears of relief brimmed over her eyes. Embarrassed by her display of emotion, she stood up, walked to the window, wiped her eyes, and gazed down at the sea-walk. In the twilight, she saw a man and woman stride briskly along the paved path. Another man with both hands clutching a walker moved behind them. Close on his heels an elderly lady's hand held a leash with a small dog on the other end. Starting to turn back to the loveseat, Philomela caught sight of a man walking briskly into view. His pace slowed as he glanced up toward Procne's unit.

Philomela gasped and quickly stepped back from the window. She hoped against hope the man hadn't seen her. If he had, he would know she and Procne were in Selene's townhome.

Tears forgotten, she dashed to the loveseat, dug her cellphone from her purse, and punched in some numbers. She sat down, held the device to her cheek, and breathlessly spoke into it.

"Constable James, Philomela Nightingale here."

The constable asked her where "here" was.

"We're at Selene Hamilton's townhouse. Procne and I are with Selene now. I just saw Roger Thistle on the sea-walk." She ignored Procne's loud gasp and listened to the voice on the other end of the phone. "Yes, that's the correct address."

Snapping her cellphone shut, she looked over at her sister, whose face registered shock and fear. The psychic's facial expression appeared calm and serene, but Philomela suspected it hid traces of terrifying fear.

"You sure it was Roger?" Procne's left hand rose as if to protect her throat.

Philomela nodded. Taking a deep breath, she tried to follow Selene's lead and appear calm. "He was on the sea-walk. He looked up and studied your condo. I hope he didn't see me, but if he did, he's aware we're here with Selene. Who knows what he'll do next? He's already killed two people and kidnapped you. Killing three more people won't matter to him." Her eyes shifted from her sister to the psychic. With an ironic smile she said, "Selene, you look like a calm, serene savior."

"I don't feel serene nor like a savior. As you said, a few more murders won't faze Roger Thistle. If he has a gun, he could blow off my door lock, come in, and finish off all three of us."

"But he still might prefer choking his victims with silk ties." Philomela tried to look wise and confident. "If that's the case, the three of us can fight him off." She stood up and started to walk to the kitchen. "Selene, where's your heaviest frying pan?"

Selene hurried after her. At a lower cupboard, she bent down and removed two frying pans and a wok. She handed the larger pan to Philomela, walked over to Procne, and handed her the smaller one. She held the wok close to her abdomen.

"We're at the ready." Philomela almost sounded like a hardened sailor. Then she giggled rather hysterically. "What a sight we are. I'd grab a butcher knife if I was confident I could use it."

"You'd hesitate," Selene said, "but Roger wouldn't."

"I'm afraid you're right. We better keep the knives out of sight." Philomela placed Selene's knife rack inside a cupboard and closed the door. Carrying the big frying pan, she sidled up to the window and peered down at the sea-walk. "Roger's no longer there. I hope he's not making his way to Selene's front door."

But it seemed he might be, for a few minutes later the doorbell rang. The three women froze like icicles hanging from an eave. They stared at each other.

"It could be Constable James," Philomela said.

Selene went to the intercom and looked at the front gate video display. "Whoever it is has ducked out of sight of the camera."

"Dickless Tracy wouldn't do that," Procne whispered.

CHAPTER 48

Tuesday Evening, Continued

The doorbell rang a second time.

"You'd better answer it," Philomela mouthed. "Pretend we're not here."

Selene swallowed a lump in her throat. "Who's there?" she asked.

"Special delivery." The voice was high but definitely male.

"From whom?" Selene asked.

"Federal Express."

"I'm not expecting anything."

"It's a small parcel."

"Don't open the gate," Philomela whispered.

The music of "Sunrise Serenade" sounded and Philomela turned, left her two cohorts gazing at the intercom screen, and ran toward Selene's spare bedroom. Inside the room, she hoped Constable James was on the other end of the phone. She said. "Hello," in a hushed tone.

"Hi, Philomela, I'm just going to board the plane in Regina. I should be in Saltaire in three hours. Will you meet me?"

"Oh, Brent. Um...yes. Of course, I'll meet you." What

else could she say? She certainly didn't want to worry him. He didn't need to fuss and fret during his flight from Regina to Saltaire.

"So, Procne got home safe and sound?" he asked.

"She and I are at Selene's right now." Then she made the understatement of the year: "We've had a bit of excitement."

"Good, you can tell me all about it when I get there."

After shutting off the cellphone, Philomela sighed, shook her head, and allowed her shoulders to droop. "What next?" she asked herself. Walking down the hall she saw Selene staring at the intercom screen.

"I still can't see anyone," Selene whispered. She shut off the intercom and looked at the two sisters. "I'm not going to let the Fed Ex guy into the vestibule."

The three women stood like statues and stared at the small black screen. Suddenly Philomela heard an ominous sound.

"Someone's at your door," she said.

"How did he get past the locked gate into the vestibule?" Procne asked.

"Maybe Sheila or Tom let him in," Selene said.

"Or maybe he somehow jimmied the lock." Philomela bit her lower lip. Hearing a scraping sound on the door she said, "Now he's trying to wreck the lock to get inside here."

They stared from one to the other for what seemed hours but was probably not even a minute. Philomela raised the large frying pan, walked to the door, and took a warrior stance. "We each have a weapon. Be prepared to use it."

Procne followed her. "Should we stand near the door and bonk him on the head the second he gets inside?"

"I think that's best," Philomela replied.

Selene tiptoed toward them. All three positioned

themselves by the door—Philomela at the doorknob side, Procne and Selene at the hinge side. They listened as the scratching noise grew louder, and they stared at the motionless doorknob.

Suddenly they heard the tune, 'Sunrise Serenade' and the scratching noise ceased.

Philomela tip-toed from the door and answered her cellphone.

"Oh, Constable James," she gasped. "I'm so glad to hear your voice. Someone got past the locked metal gate and is in the vestibule trying to unlock the door to Selene's townhouse. We're terrified."

"We're one block away," the constable replied. "We'll be there in a couple of minutes."

Closing her cellphone, Philomela hoped the police would get here before the murderer killed all three of them. She clutched the frying pan tightly and tip-toed back to her cohorts. As she re-took position, she saw the doorknob move. She held her breath, prepared for the worst. If Roger opened the door, she would be the first to be shot—if he had a gun. If he didn't have a gun—she was ready. She raised the large frying pan high in the air, prepared to crash it on his head.

The door opened quickly and she did exactly that. She hit the intruder on the head. It momentarily stunned him, but he recovered quickly. He took a step toward her, and Selene stepped forward and swung the wok at his head, but he shifted position and the pan smashed his shoulder. Procne stepped up and whammed his head with the small frying pan. His eyes widened in apparent surprise, and his body slowly slid to the floor.

Philomela stared at him and hoped he would stay unconscious for a long time. To her relief, she heard the sound of running feet outside and the words, "Police." She ran to the metal gate. It was not damaged, so Tom or

Sheila must have let Roger through it. With relief, she said to the police, "You're just in time. Come on in."

After Roger Arthur Thistle was taken away, Corporal Stinson and Constable James sat down with the three women in Selene's sitting area. The police praised the women's presence of mind and their abilities to cope with what could have been a fatal situation.

"According to the profiling," Corporal Stinson said, "Roger was being a successful realtor by eliminating his competition. Kathy and Annette were threats to him because they were so efficient and so well-liked. He was not as well-liked, and he was not prepared to work as hard as they did. Procne, though you're not a realtor, you piqued his envy because you were another well-liked, hard-working, successful young female. In all three instances, his envy fell into a pit of unjustifiable revenge. Your sister rescued you from that shack in the nick of time."

Procne's dark blue eyes caught Philomela's green ones and her head nodded a silent thank you.

CHAPTER 49

A Week Later.

Philomela sat in the passenger seat of the red truck, looked at the long line of cars waiting to board the ferry, and thought of the forthcoming ordeal of moving.

First, she would get rid of some of their worldly goods—maybe at a garage sale, but more likely as donations to a second hand thrift shop. Then she'd pack up the items they wanted to take to their house in Saltaire. Moving would be labor intensive, but eliminating unneeded stuff would reduce some of the stress.

For almost the hundredth time, Brent shook his head. "I can't believe what you went through while I was away. If I'd realized that Procne was in such danger, I never would have gone to Saskatchewan."

"Brent, don't beat yourself up. Nobody expected Procne to be kidnapped."

"The killer sure fooled me. I didn't suspect him at all."

"Neither did any of us. At first."

The cars ahead started to move and Brent slowly drove his truck on the ramp over open water and onto the ferry's car deck. Stopping, he turned off the engine.

Philomela sighed. "In another month we'll be Procne's permanent pests."

"She'll like it." Brent turned to his wife. "I just hope the town of Saltaire is humdrum and boring. I also hope you never again are involved with a murder."

Philomela smiled at him. "Well, would you agree we should never say never?"

The End

About the Author

Benni Chisholm grew up on the Canadian prairies and, while a student earning a BSN, started writing light verse. Later, in the shadows of the Rocky Mountain foothills she worked as a public health nurse, helped four wonderful children raise themselves, and saw the publication of a few poems, a biography, an anniversary booklet, a newsletter (eight years as editor), and several articles and short stories. Now she and her husband enjoy life in the Pacific Northwest. Chisholm's fondness for travel is apparent in her two mystery novels: *Stained Sand*, which is set in Hawaii, and *Odd Odyssey*, where the protagonist finds adventure on a trip around the world.